# WELCOME TO WACKY WATER WORLD

## Edania Chronicles: Book 3

Matthew S Porter

ISBN: 9798720620851

Cover design by: Jenny Ahern (Instagram: @aeonpigments)

Published by Matthew Porter
https://matthewporterauthor.com

# DEDICATION

To Amanda, one of my closest friends. Without you, this series would not be where it is now.

# CONTENTS


Acknowledgments i

Doren Report #5—Marina Pg 3

1 Freezing Cold—Abby Pg 12

2 Gabrielle—Abby Pg 27

3 Waterpark Recon—Abby Pg 38

4 Tunnel of Love—Kelly Pg 53

5 Rough Waters Ahead—Kelly Pg 69

6 Drowning—Abby Pg 88

7 F.E.S.P.A. Returns—Abby Pg 100

8 Wacky Water Tower—Abby Pg 114

Doren Report #6—On Dark-Segols—Reality Benders Pg 131

9 Brothers—James Pg 142

10 Top of the Tower—James Pg 161

11 Torn Tower—Abby Pg 177

12 Rainy Days—Abby Pg 191

# ACKNOWLEDGMENTS

Big shoutout to Natasja and Amanda for working with me every step of the way. Without you, this would definitely not be possible. For Jenny as well, for her awesome job with the artwork and cover.

# DOREN REPORT #5—MARINA



"So, Barbaas is dead, is he?" Doren asked from his virtual prison. "Are you sure, Flutura?"

Flutura bowed before the computer. "Yes, Master." She looked up at him, feigning sorrow. "When I reached the submerged power plant, the Edanian agents had already caused the Illusion Tree to fall, and Barbaas was crushed under its fractured roots, his body burned from the explosion. There was no saving him. All I could do was acquire the Ark." She held out a round, flat object with a glimmering yellow jewel in the middle of it.

"So, it was the Ark that caused the disturbance to the lair's power?" Doren asked.

"Indeed it was," Flutura answered. "These objects contain such power, the depths of which we cannot even fathom."

"Then, we must handle it with care," said Doren. "Well done, Flutura. Place the Ark on the pedestal under the screen."

Flutura walked to the computer screen and put the Ark on the pedestal right below it. A glass dome closed around it, and the computer analyzed it. The lights in the room began to flicker.

Doren laughed madly. "Excellent! I can feel the barrier keeping me in here weakening from the Ark's power. We just need the other six and I'll be free."

Flutura smiled sweetly. "I'm on it, Master. I will gather the remaining Arks and deliver them to you and—" She shivered as a single drop of water fell onto her forehead. She looked up at the ceiling. Another drop of water dripped on her. Then another.

*Drip…drip…drip.*

"What is this?" Doren snapped as more water began to fall.

Flutura tried to find the source. "I don't know, Master. Perhaps there was a pipe that burst from above when the Ark caused the power outage."

"That's not it," a man's voice said from behind Flutura.

"Balthazar," said Flutura as the dripping became a steady flow.

Balthazar appeared from the shadows, his face obscured by his black cloak. "This water is emitting a Dark-Segol energy signature."

The flow turned into a heavy downpour.

"What is the meaning of this?" yelled Doren.

The torrential downpour suddenly stopped, and all of the water flowed to the central control room's entrance, forming a large puddle. With a loud roar, a powerful geyser shot out of it.

"I do not mean to intrude, Master Doren. I assure you, I come in peace," said a soft, feminine voice from inside the torrent.

The geyser opened up elegantly like a liquid rose, and there stood a young woman. She was slender and petite, and had long, jet black hair in a bun surrounded by a vine of blue hydrangea flowers. Her eyes were azure like the sea. Her skin was pale like the moon. She was wearing a furisode kimono that was deep blue with black trim.

"Who are you that you would intrude into *my* lair?" Doren growled.

The woman gracefully trod to the computer screen and bowed. "My name is Marina, and I've come to help with your quest to gather the Arks."

"And how do *you* know of our plans for the Arks?" Flutura snapped.

Marina glanced at her and smiled kindly. "Everyone knows of Master Doren's plan. It's not much of a secret among the Corrupted."

Balthazar suddenly appeared behind her and grabbed the back of her neck. "And tell me, little mermaid, from what vile pool did you flop out of?"

A smile remained on her face as Balthazar's grip grew stronger. "If you please," she said in an eerily calm manner. Her body liquified and poured out of Balthazar's grip, then seeped into the ground. A pillar of water shot up from behind him and solidified back into the lovely young woman. "I have been training with Madame Circe of the Olympian Alliance for quite some time. But I left just hours ago when I heard that my dear sister had been brutally murdered by the Edania Organization's new agents."

"That repugnant flower child was your sister?" asked Flutura, as the thought of the wretch filled her entire being with hatred.

Marina's eyes became cold as she glared at Flutura. Then her face became as serene as a calm sea. "Thistle was my sister, yes. I've come to avenge her untimely and embarrassing demise."

"You have no right to interfere with our plans!" Flutura snapped.

Marina frowned. "Please, mind your temper. It's quite unseemly for a woman as beautiful as you. I am simply here to offer my services to Master Doren, and in doing so, get my revenge on the Edania Organization. I assure you, I am quite competent, and I have excellent references."

Balthazar sneered. "Nobody at the Olympian Alliance should be called an excellent *anything*. They all betrayed Master Doren in his time of need."

"Oh, dear, no. I'm not referring to them," said Marina, shaking her head.

"She's talking about me," echoed a very deep, hollow voice.

"So, we have more unexpected guests..." said Doren, trying not to get enraged at the presumptuousness of it all.

A thick, dark fog descended upon the room, and a cloaked figure appeared from its midst. "You're not being very hospitable, Doren. Being trapped in your own computer is no excuse for such rudeness."

Flutura took a moth-shaped shuriken from her belt. "How *dare* you speak to Master Doren in such a manner! I ought to cut your tongue out!"

Balthazar quickly grabbed her hand and lowered it. "Don't," he said flatly.

On the computer screen, Doren's shadowy figure took a step back. "M-Master Faust…my apologies. I didn't realize it was you."

Shock and horror filled Flutura as she watched the dark figure approaching. "Did he just call that man in the hood 'Master'?" she whispered to Balthazar.

Balthazar didn't utter a word, or even acknowledge her question. He stood as still as death, glaring at the man robed in black.

The man turned to Flutura. "Indeed he did, my dear," he said in a pleasant tone. "My name is Faust. I am what is known as a Recruiter, much like the brilliant young Balthazar there."

Balthazar bowed. "Th-thank you, sir. Although I'm nowhere near as brilliant as you are."

*Did Balthazar just bow down to someone?* Flutura thought. "You're a Recruiter…like Balthazar?" she said out loud.

Faust nodded. "I am. In fact, I'm the oldest surviving Recruiter among all of the Corrupted. I'm the one that brought Balthazar into the darkness. I'm also responsible for recruiting Doren."

Flutura quickly put her shuriken away and bowed her head. "Forgive my insolence. I had no idea."

"I will forgive it this time," Faust said pleasantly. "You didn't know to whom you were speaking. Now then." He turned his attention to Doren's pixelated image. "I must insist that you let Marina aid you in getting the next Ark, Doren. She and Thistle were my most promising new recruits, but poor Thistle was cut down before she could really master her power. That said, I wish to give Marina a chance to exercise her Dark-Segol and kill those foolish agents for her sister's sake."

Marina held her hand out, and a luminous orb of water appeared above it. "I assure you, I am a very skilled water manipulator. I can create illusions with my water, much like Thistle could with her plants. And, although her illusions packed more of an offensive punch, mine are much more stable and almost impossible to escape once my victims become ensnared."

Flutura grunted in anger. It looked like once again, her mission would be stripped of her.

Marina glanced over at Flutura and smiled. "Please don't be too upset, dear. I know my sister's personality was a bit...abrasive. I tried to make her more of a lady, but I suppose she was not granted our mother's grace and charm like I was. I welcome any help I can get."

Flutura turned her back on Marina. "There is no need for that. I have my own project to work on. I *truly* wish you luck on collecting the Ark," she said as she stormed out of the central control room.

"My, my, my. Why is it that most of the female Corrupteds these days are so brutish?" Marina chimed. "Just because we don't have our humanity doesn't mean we've lost our ability to be civilized."

"That's enough of that, Marina," said Faust.

Marina bowed regally. "My apologies."

"Now," said Faust as he turned his attention back to Doren. "My dear Marina has already found the Ark, and she has a plan to gather the energy to shatter its defenses."

Marina nodded. "Yes, the Ark is in an abandoned water bottling plant, ironically enough."

"Tell them your plan, Marina," Faust instructed.

She giggled. "Yes, of course." The glowing ball of water dripped onto her hand, and her whole arm became a stream of water. "My entire body can turn to water, but it's no ordinary water. Every drop is infused with Malkirite. My plan is to reopen this bottling factory and sell the ignorant citizens of the Force-Pointe Islands bottles of water infused with my dark energy. When they drink the water, it will slowly drain their life-energy without them even knowing. And since the water is from my body, all that energy will come back to me, and I'll apply it to the Ark's barrier."

"What if the children from the Edania Organization come sniffing around?" asked Doren.

She seemed unphased. "Like I said, my water can also create illusions. Well, it's a little more complex than that. To be more precise, my water can create an inescapable dimension of illusions. If they interfere with my plan, I will simply trap and kill them in there. Oh, I do hope they interfere. I very much look forward to drowning them in an ocean of sorrow," she giggled.

Faust cackled. "Quite the young lady, wouldn't you agree, Doren? While being forever the polite debutant outwardly, on the inside she's wickedly devious."

Marina scoffed. "I most certainly am *not* devious. I just wish to do away with those self-righteous rapscallions."

"If the opportunity comes, seize it. But be warned," said Doren.

Marina looked up at the computer screen with a frown.

"Do not seek these agents out," he continued. "Or purposely draw them in. They may be mere children, but they've been able to best one of my most loyal servants, as well as your very own sister. It would be unwise for you to underestimate them."

Her eyes sharpened as she stared at Doren. She managed a thin smile. "There is no need to worry, sir. I will not be bested. Rest assured, I will be completely focused on obtaining the Ark for you."

"By the way, do you know which Ark it is?" asked Balthazar.

"I believe it is Jordan's Ark," Faust answered.

Balthazar pondered. "Jordan… Which of the agents was that?"

Doren huffed. "She was the one that could stop time… What an annoying little power. They have a time-stopper in this group, too."

Marina picked one of the flowers out of her hair and stared at it longingly. "If it's the time-freezer that will be contending for the Ark, that's good news for me."

"How is that good news for anyone?" asked Balthazar.

Marina slowly turned around to face Balthazar, twirling as if she were at a ball. She crushed the flower in her hands, smiling wickedly. "Let's just say that I won't be easy to freeze inside of anything, let alone something as insignificant as time."

Balthazar looked at her in disbelief. "Tch, are you saying you're immune to her time-stopping Segol? That's quite unusual for a Corrupted of your rank."

She looked at him graciously. "I'm not saying anything, love. You'll just have to watch as I mop the floor with her and her foolish little friends." She put her hand over her mouth and blushed. "Oops, that was not very ladylike. I apologize."

Balthazar sighed. "Some other time, perhaps. I'm afraid I've got to go. Lots of evil things to do, so little time. Is there anything else you needed of me, Master Doren? Master Faust?"

"No, Balthazar. You may leave," said Doren.

"It was good seeing you, my apprentice," said Faust.

Balthazar nodded, and disappeared into the shadows.

"I truly hope Balthazar is pleasing you, Doren," Faust said. "Has he brought in any good followers?"

Doren nodded. "Yes, I am quite pleased with his work. He's delivered a few good subordinates, and his skill of shadow manipulation is also quite useful. You trained him well."

"Yes," Faust said. "He was one of my favorite projects, much like Marina and her family. But she has little interest in being a Recruiter like me or Balthazar."

Marina put both hands into the opposite sleeves. "You're quite right. I don't want to find people to follow others. I wish to find my own subjects that will follow my every command. At any rate, I think I shall take my leave."

"Very well," Faust said. "Go and wreak some havoc, young one."

She looked offended. "I am a lady. I do not *wreak* anything. I'll nurture and care for said havoc until fully developed, then I'll let it bloom over all of these islands and enjoy the wails of sorrow like a symphony of death." She giggled. "Well, goodbye for now. I will not disappoint you." She bowed, then quickly vanished behind a pillar of water.

Faust turned back to Doren. "I believe I will go, too. I have a new group of people I'm working with for recruitment. Unfortunately, most of them are fools, but one truly shows promise. I'll see you soon, old friend—hopefully next time you'll be out of your computer prison."

"Farewell, Master Faust," Doren said with a bow.

Faust disappeared in a puff of dark smoke.

* * *

Flutura was pacing in her chambers. "Ooh, that wretched fish out of water! 'I'm such a lady, I'm going to let you help.' Well, I'd like to help, alright, help her dry up like a fish in the desert."

Balthazar rose from the ground. "Do not fret, my sweet," he said as he went to her.

She stepped away from him. "I'm not in the mood to see you, Balthazar. I want to be left alone."

He held out a dead rose. "Please don't be upset, my wicked little moth."

She turned away from him. "Too late! This is the third time I've been overlooked. The Ark retrieval mission is supposed to be mine!"

"You'll have your time to shine, don't you worry."

"Not with the obnoxious mermaid here. Ugh, no matter. Now I can focus my work on *her*."

"*Her?*" repeated Balthazar. "Are you referring to whatever you have in your lab that you won't let me see?"

"Yes," she answered. "And I promise you that when I'm finished with my project, I will not be ignored again!"

# CHAPTER 1: FREEZING COLD—ABBY

It was the week after we just barely made it out of Hotel Barbaas with our lives, and we were still licking our wounds. James was upset because he felt like he had been outsmarted by the bad guys; Kelly was mad because they'd gotten away with the Ark that was supposed to be hers; Nick was brooding all week because he didn't think he'd done a good job as the leader. And me? Well, I was totally done with the whole thing. We all put on our happy faces as we walked into school Tuesday morning, but in truth, I was sick of it all…literally.

"*Achoo!*" I sneezed, and not too gracefully, either.

Nick jumped away from my line of fire. "Jeez, Abbs, watch where you're sprayin'," he said as we walked to homeroom.

"Ugh, sorry," I said as I took a tissue out of my pocket and blew my nose. "I've had this stupid cold since the outdoor pep rally Saturday night."

James's face got paler than usual. "Y-you're sick?" he said as put his shirt over his nose.

Kelly rolled her eyes. "Well, James is going to be out of commission for the next several hours."

James dug through his backpack and took a can of disinfectant spray out and started to spray all over the place. "Die, you filthy germs!" he yelled.

"I'm sorry, James… I didn't mean to make you go totally psycho," I said.

To tell you the truth, I was a little offended. I mean, it's not like I had Ebola!

He continued to spray. "It's quite alright, just keep your distance." I guess he was going to treat me like a leper until I was over this cold.

"I never get sick," I protested. "It must be the stress… I mean, first we were down in that basement with all of those nasty bugs, then we were in the woods with all of the freaky plants, *and then* we got trapped in a hotel that was really a man-eating tree. Oh yeah, add those giant spiders and other bugs and the fact that we were almost blown up—not to mention Alyssa's torturous gymnastics practices *and* the stupid pre-basketball season pep rally over the weekend."

Nick interjected. "Hey, it wasn't stupid. I worked all afternoon to get everything set up. Coach Isely couldn't get anyone else to do it."

"You had *some* help, Nick," Kelly said, sounding totally passive-aggressive. "Alyssa and her peacocks were cheering you on from the sidelines…the whole time."

"Really?" he said innocently. "I didn't notice." He was probably telling the truth. My brother could be a little dense when it came to people crushing on him.

Kelly huffed. "I'm sure you didn't. You were just hard at work."

Nick smiled at her. "By the way, Kelly, thanks for helping me with the decorations. I'm no good at stuff like that."

"That was pretty apparent," she answered with a snicker.

We walked into homeroom and sat down.

"When is the first basketball game, by the way?" asked Kelly.

"On Friday," said Nick. "Weren't you paying attention at the rally?"

*She was too busy being mad at Alyssa*, I thought.

"You guys are coming, right?" Nick asked.

"I'm your sister, I have to come," I answered, already feeling the migraine.

"I wouldn't miss it," Kelly said sincerely.

"I will attend as well, as long as I don't die from the plague first," said James, still holding his shirt to his nose.

Kelly licked her hand and placed it on James's forehead.

James leaped out of his desk. "*K-Kelly*," he said shrilly. "Wh-why would you do that?"

She looked at him disapprovingly like she was his mom. "Because you're being ridiculous, James. Abby has a cold, not anthrax."

James pulled out a pack of alcohol wipes and wiped his forehead.

"How much disinfectant do you have in that bag?" I asked, watching him being totally OCD.

"Oh, just your standards," he answered. "I have disinfectant spray, alcohol wipes, hand sanitizer just in case I can't get to the sink. I have some antibacterial ointment, antibacterial adhesive bandages, medical-grade iodine—"

"Why in the world do you have iodine?" asked Kelly as her eyebrows shot to the ceiling. I don't know why she was surprised, though. This was James we were talking about.

James looked shocked and insulted. "What kind of question is that? The better question is, why doesn't *everyone* have iodine in their backpacks?"

She took a deep breath. "One of these days, I really hope you realize how crazy you sound."

"Alright, everyone. Take your seats," Mrs. Snider said as she walked into the room.

James quickly sat back down, still covering his nose with his collar.

Mrs. Snider walked to her desk. "Now, before first period begins, I want to pass your tests back. I apologize that it took so long, but I figured that I would wait 'til everyone that was absent from the insect infestation finished their tests. Overall, I'm a little disappointed," she said as she started to hand back the tests.

"Aw, man…" said Nick. "If I bombed this test, I won't be able to be in the first game. I studied so hard, too."

Jeremy DeGallo looked back at him. "Nobody expected you to do well, pretty boy," he said smugly. Jeremy was the leader of what James liked to call the Hyena Gang, a bunch of jerks that loved to make everyone's lives miserable. While his lackies were all big and dumb, Jeremy was shrewd and scrawny. "Remember when you said you did better than me?" he continued. "Clearly it was all talk."

Nick clenched his jaw.

"Don't worry, you haven't even gotten your test back yet," I said, trying to calm him down.

Jeremy got his test back, and his face turned red. He pulled on Mrs. Snider's sleeve to get her attention. "Um, I think you mis-graded here, Mrs. Snider," he tried to whisper. "It says that I got an eighty-two."

Mrs. Snider pulled her arm away from his grip. "I don't mis-grade, Jeremy. That's your score. Definitely not your best."

She got to the back and handed us our tests.

I was pleasantly surprised. "Sweet, I got a ninety-two."

"Same here," said Kelly, showing me her test.

Mrs. Snider flipped Nick's test over on his desk like she was trying to hide it. Disappointment was painted on his face as he looked up at her. "How'd I do, Mrs. S? I don't really wanna look at the test score."

She frowned. "You're just going to have to take a look for yourself."

Nick slowly flipped the page over. "Woah, I got a ninety-five?"

She grinned. "Looks like it. From now on I expect nothing less from you, Nicklaus."

Nick held the test up to show James. "J-Man, I got a ninety-five!"

James examined his test. "Well done. I told you that you could do it."

Mrs. Snider gave James his test and walked to the front without saying a word.

James looked at his test and almost passed out.

"What is it, James?" Kelly asked.

"I—I got…" He could hardly speak.

Kelly's eyes got wide. "Got what?"

"I got a…" He was starting to hyperventilate.

"It can't be that bad," I said.

He took his glasses off and started to rock. "It *is* that bad! This is the worst thing that's ever happened to me… I got…I got a…I got a ninety-nine!"

Kelly rolled her eyes. "That's still a very high A."

He looked at her like she was some kind of monster. "I've never gotten anything lower than a perfect on a science test! I'm ruined. I suppose I should get used to the idea of working at a…fast food restaurant for the rest of my life."

Nick chuckled. "You just congratulated me on a ninety-five. How could you be freaking out with a ninety-nine?"

His breathing calmed down a little bit. "Biology is not your passion… How would you feel if you scored one hundred *goals* in basketball your whole life, but the next game you score less?"

"Baskets, J-Man," Nick corrected. "They're called baskets. And I'm not *that* good at basketball, but I guess I get your point."

"What question did you miss?" asked Kelly.

He looked at his test like it was a subpoena or something. "One of the identification questions… I put eosinophil when it was clearly a basophil. How could I be so blind?"

"I got that question wrong, too," said Kelly.

"Me too," I said.

Nick grinned ear to ear. "Not me. That was one I got right!"

James groaned and banged his head on the desk. "I am the worst intellectual who has ever lived… I don't deserve to be in the Edania Organization. I am supposed to be the tactician, but I got a ninety-nine on my biology test. It's no wonder I got bested by Thistle and Barbaas."

Nick patted him on the back. "Don't beat yourself up, buddy. You figured out how to beat that Thistle chick. You did good. It's me who's the loser in that department."

"Nick—" I said angrily. "How many times do I have to tell you that it's not your fault?"

He looked at me and frowned. "But I'm the leader, and we almost lost J-Man *and* Kelly. It's a good thing J-Man was able to outsmart the bad guys and Steph does that thing that cancels out other superpowers. It was a mess, and we lost the Ark."

"I have to take the blame there," said Kelly. "I could have grabbed it, but I didn't."

I chimed in. "If we're playing the blame game, I blame myself, too. I could have been a lot more help if I just knew how to control my freezing power and—" I glanced around, and everyone was staring at us.

"We're… Talking about an RPG," James said, nervously. "It was a rough campaign."

I glared at him. *Omigosh. I am so not the kind of person that plays those things! Now all the guys in class are gonna think I'm some kind of megadork!*

But nobody seemed to care, because they just turned around and continued their own conversations.

"Alright, everyone," Mrs. Snider said. "It's time for class, so get out your books and turn to chapter thirty-three."

Second period was chemistry. That day we were experimenting with liquid nitrogen, something that could freeze almost anything. But not time…so, I guess I had it beat.

After chem was English, which was one subject I actually enjoyed. I sat down in the back, and Alyssa DeGallo, Jeremy's annoying sister and captain of the gymnastics team, sat in front of me, much to my displeasure. She turned around and flicked her hair.

"So, Abby, you know we're BFFs, right?" she said in a super cheery voice.

"Since when?" I asked, kinda wanting to vomit at the thought.

She giggled. "Since forevs, silly! And BFFs help out their friends when they're in need, right?"

I raised my eyebrow. "Uh, we aren't even remotely friends. You've always had a problem with me."

She laughed loudly. "Silly Abby, I just tease you 'cause that's what friends do!" She was so full of crap.

"What do you want?" I asked, not really caring about the answer.

She placed her elbows on my desk and rested her head on her hands. "All I want is for you to tell me everything about Nicky poo."

"Nicky poo?" I repeated. The desire to vomit just got a lot stronger.

She laughed loudly again. "Yeah, that's the nickname I gave him. Isn't it cute?" *Somebody, please shut her up.* "At least answer me this—is he single?"

I didn't answer; I was too busy focusing on not yacking all over my desk.

She grabbed my hand, but I quickly took it back. "C'mon, Abby," she said. "It's time for girl talk. He's not interested in that prude Kelly Azusa, is he? She's so backward, and don't even get me started about her outfit choices! But Nicky does spend a lot of time with her, and that loser Dr. Stumpenstein—"

Now I was getting mad. "James isn't a loser. He's actually pretty cool…in his own weird kind of way. As far as Kelly is concerned, I don't know if he's interested in her or not. That's something to ask him. But don't talk about my actual friends like that. Truth be told, even if Nick was interested in you, I'd make sure to talk him out of it."

She hmphed. "Don't be so nasty, jeez." She turned around and flicked her flaxen hair in my face. "It's clear that Nick got all of the nice *and* the hot genes in your family."

*I really hope that someday we discover that she's an undercover Corrupted so we can teach her a lesson, the painted-up witch!*

Mr. McGee, the English teacher, walked into the room. He was short, middle aged and balding. He was totally one of the cool teachers, one of my favorites. "Alright, guys. Let's pick up where we left off on our discussion of *The Crucible*. Now, what did you think of Abigail Williams?"

Alyssa raised her hand.

"Yes, Alyssa?" Mr. McGee said as he nodded to her.

She obnoxiously twirled her hair while she talked. "Yeah, so, I actually like her. All except for her name… Personally, I think the name Abigail is just so…blah." Yeah, real subtle there.

"What made you like her character?" asked Mr. McGee, genuinely surprised at her answer.

"She's just trying to get what she wants," Alyssa said obnoxiously. "And in a society of stuck-up colonists, it's nice to see a girl with that much boldness."

I sighed. Apparently too loudly, because Mr. McGee looked at me. "Abby, what do you think?"

I folded my hands. "I don't like her…except for her name. I mean, she was falsely accusing people of witchcraft to get what she wanted, going so far as to point her finger at her lover's wife, knowing that she'll get hanged."

Alyssa scoffed. "Yeah, only if she denied being a witch."

I rebutted. "But she wasn't really a witch, and Abigail Williams and the rest of the girls in Salem were just being cruel for their own gain, or the gain of their families."

Alyssa raised her hands defensively. "Don't get so offended. This is all just a work of fiction anyway."

"Well, this is turning out to be an interesting discussion," Mr. McGee said, nodding. "Anyone else have some input?" He pointed to Sara Hay, one of the more agreeable girls from the gymnastics team.

"Yeah, I think that everyone in Salem is psychotic," she said.

I could feel my nose start to tickle. I quickly grabbed for a tissue out of my bookbag.

Mr. McGee chuckled. "Interesting choice of words… Why do you think that?"

I barely made it to my tissue. I sneezed and almost sprayed the back of Alyssa's head.

Sara started. "Just look at how—" She stopped talking, and the whole room went dead quiet.

In a panic, I looked around. I was the only one in the room that was moving. Great…I just Freeze-Framed the entire class when I sneezed!

There was absolutely no movement in the room; even the clock on the wall stopped ticking. I got out of my chair, ran to the door and looked out the window into the hall, where I saw a few students walking down the hallway.

*Good, they're not frozen. But what if someone walks in? What if someone sees that I'm the only one moving? They'll know that I'm responsible! Calm down, Abby. Just breathe. You know you tend to panic, and panicking can make things worse. Just sit down before they unfreeze.*

I walked back to my desk and sat down, and a second later everyone in the room started moving again.

"—crazy everyone's acting as everything's going on. It's like the entire community collapsed from all of the hysteria," Sara finished.

Mr. McGee smiled. "Good input. And it makes sense that these girls who, according to puritan society were to be seen and not heard, would act brashly when given such authority over the town's court. According to the council, they were the fingers of judgment, given the power to point out the hidden evils of the world. Now, how do you think any of you would react if you were suddenly given power from on high, so to speak?"

I rolled my eyes. *I have* been given power from on high, teach, in a much more literal sense. My friends and I are using our powers to fight the actual hidden evils of the world. You don't see us pointing our fingers at people we don't like.

The bell rang for class to be over.

Mr. McGee looked at the clock and blinked. "Hmm, that's weird. The clock must be a little off. Anyway, good job everyone, and have a good rest of your day."

Fourth period was social studies, which was another class I enjoyed. Mrs. Crowe was the social studies teacher, and she kept things interesting. She would hold Socratic seminars, meaning she would get us all in a circle and ask us the questions and have us answer, sort of like a reverse lecture. Everyone had to give two acceptable answers; after that they were good for the rest of the class.

"Okay, so what does the term *checks and balances* mean?" asked Mrs. Crowe.

I raised my hand.

"Yes, Abby?"

"In this case, the term refers to the fact that every branch of government is…" I felt a tickle in my nose.

Mrs. Crowe looked at me, waiting for me to finish my answer.

"Every branch of…government—" *Oh no, here it comes.* "Ev— Achoo!" I sneezed, and everyone in the room froze, just like in English.

"Great!" I yelled. *This is getting ridiculous! Is this going to happen every time I sneeze? Why can't I control this ability? The others have, more or less. I thought I was getting the hang of it, but I guess I was wrong. I would at least like to unfreeze the room whenever I want, but noooo.*

I sat there and waited for everything to mobilize again. When the room unfroze, Mrs. Crowe said, "Bless you."

"Thank you," I muttered. *Alright, they were frozen for about a minute, give or take a second or two. I think that's a little less than in English.*

"Now, how about those checks and balances?" Mrs. Crowe asked, looking at me expectantly.

"Oh, right," I said. "It ensures that every branch of government isn't given too much power. So, if the president tries to pass something, it has to go by the Supreme Court and Congress. Each branch of government has divided authority."

"Good job, Abby," she said.

Well, I had an extra minute to think up the answer, not that I could think clearly with all of the panic.

During lunch, I tried to voice my frustrations to the others.

"Hmm, you Freeze-Framed the entire class?" asked James, who was keeping his distance from me.

"Twice," I said, trying to hold in my panic. "Once in English, the other in social studies. Honestly, it's getting pretty— *Achoo!*" I hesitated to open my eyes. I didn't want to see the entire lunchroom Freeze-Framed. But I could still hear the sounds of people talking. I opened my eyes and saw that everyone was still moving, much to my relief.

Nick looked around. "Welp, it looks like you're not having that problem now."

"It's most likely because we're in a large room with too many people," said James, who was now standing behind the pillar next to the lunch table. "You couldn't stop time right now even if you wanted to."

It sounded weird, but I was perfectly happy with my superpower's limitations. I sighed with relief and opened my carton of orange juice and started to chug it to help with my cold.

Kirsten Ferdinand, a girl from homeroom, walked up to the lunch table. "Hey, Abby, orange juice won't get the job done as fast as this." She handed me a very colorful bottle of water with the image of a laughing watermelon.

I read the label. "Wacky Water? I've never heard of it."

"It's new," she said, sounding a little too excited. "There's this old water factory near Soraya Woods that just reopened, and it's been manufacturing Wacky Water. This stuff's great, it's all flavored and has a bunch of vitamins and minerals."

"Thanks, but I really don't like watermelon-flavored stuff," I said, giving her the bottle back.

She smiled. "They have a ton of flavors. They just installed a vending machine for it down the hall."

"Maybe I'll go get some," I said.

She pointed at the TV on the wall. "Oh, there's something about it on the news!"

The entire lunchroom went quiet. I looked around, and it seemed like almost everyone in the room was drinking this Wacky Water stuff, and they all seemed entranced by the TV.

On the TV, the news anchor was talking to a pretty young woman who was wearing a blue kimono with wave patterns on it. "We're here live at the newly opened Wacky Water factory with its owner, Miss—"

"Marina, just call me Marina," the woman in the kimono interrupted. Her long hair was pinned up with two cyan chopsticks, and she had a wreath of gorgeous blue flowers on her head.

The news lady nodded. "So, Marina, tell us a little bit about this Wacky Water."

Marina looked at the camera and smiled. Her expression was warm and kind, but her sapphire eyes looked as cold as ice. "Of course. I came across this sorry water factory a short time ago, and I decided to buy and reopen it. Water is definitely a passion of mine, and I've been working to perfect bottled water to make it tasty and more nutritious. I've developed a secret formula that infuses water with many wonderful flavors. And, my water has some rather unique properties, but I don't wish to bore everyone with the details."

The news anchor seemed impressed. "So, I hear you also want to announce some exciting news pertaining to this Wacky Water that's been taking the Force-Pointe Islands by storm?"

Marina giggled. "Yes, and it's exciting news indeed. Within the factory grounds, we have recently constructed a water park called Wacky Water World. The grand opening is tomorrow afternoon, and admission is free for tomorrow only. We're also giving everyone in the park free Wacky Water."

"Wow, that certainly is generous," said the news lady.

Marina nodded. "Well, I just know that the consumers will certainly give back for such hospitality."

"Well, there you have it," the anchor said. "I definitely know where I'm going to be tomorrow."

Marina looked straight at the camera. Her gaze was serene, but there was something totally wrong about it that I couldn't quite put my finger on. "Come one, come all to the grand opening of Wacky Water World. I guarantee that you'll spend all of your energy on the fun and exciting attractions."

"Hmm, that water factory has been abandoned since I can remember…" said James, who was still standing away from the lunch table. "And there has been no sign of construction or anything around there. That factory is near Soraya Woods. We should have noticed *something* when we were there for our, ahem, *internship*."

"I guess they've just been doing it in secret," Kirsten suggested. "It sounds like fun, so I'm definitely going!"

James started rubbing his forehead. "Ugh…"

"Um, is he okay?" asked Kirsten.

"Yeah, he's just prone to headaches sometimes," said Kelly.

James snapped out of it a moment later and looked up at the TV. "Yes, I think we should go to this…Wacky Water World, too," he said suddenly.

*Oh, great. He probably saw where the next Ark is…but it hasn't even been a week, can't we get some kind of break?*

"*You* want to go to a water park?" Kirsten asked him, crossing her arms.

"Yes," he answered. "I believe it will be an interesting experience for me."

She smiled at him. "Good for you, getting over your germaphobia." Like okay, did she not see him cowering like a baby when I sneezed? "Anyway, I'll see you guys later." Kirsten walked away, chugging her Wacky Water.

James cringed. "It has nothing to do with my germaphobia. It's not like I am going to step foot in the water with everyone… So unsanitary, they don't make bleach strong enough to—"

"So did'ja see the next Ark or somethin', J-Man?" Nick interrupted.

He fixed his glasses. "Indeed, why else would I suggest going somewhere as disgusting as a water park? It certainly isn't for the *cryptosporidium* that's probably in the water."

"So, what exactly did you see to make you think the Ark is there?" asked Kelly.

James thought for a moment. "I saw some sort of factory with vats of water everywhere, then I saw the Ark. I believe that this Wacky Water World is likely the location. It is highly suspicious for a water park to show up overnight, and for this bottling plant to be fully functional after it's been in disrepair for years… I think something *froggy* is going on here."

"I think you mean fishy," I corrected.

He looked at me and blinked. "Isn't that what I said?"

"Well, it looks like our third mission has officially started. I'm pumped!"

said Nick, standing up from his chair.

"Sit down," I said, tugging on his shirt. "You're so embarrassing." *Why is he so excited, anyway? It's not like our last mission went well. I have a bad feeling about this.*

# CHAPTER 2: GABRIELLE—ABBY

"*Achoo!* Oh no… Did I freeze anyone?" I asked, not wanting to look for myself as we walked to history.

"Naw, you're good, Abbs," Nick answered.

"Ugh!" I yelled in frustration. "This is driving me crazy!"

"As long as we stay in big, open spaces you should be okay," said Kelly, trying to sound reassuring.

I crossed my arms. "What would be better is if I didn't have to worry about accidentally Freeze-Framing people at all."

"This is a fascinating manifestation of illness," James said, writing in his notebook as we walked. "I wonder if everyone with a Segol has to worry about their abilities going on the fritz if they're sick, or if this side effect would only affect neophytes like us?"

Kelly got close to James. "Do you want to run an experiment, James? You can be the next test subject. Hey, Abby, why don't you sneeze on him so we can get this experiment started?"

"Absolutely not, Kelly!" James yelled as he backed ten paces behind us. "A simple case of the common cold is one thing, but I do not want my Segol to go haywire if I get sick. Aside from the typical headaches due to illness, the ones I would get from my Scan ability on top of that would probably kill me."

She laughed. "I was just kidding."

"Well, it was not humorous at all!" he yelled up to her.

Something I noticed right away as we walked into history class was that everyone was drinking Wacky Water, and I mean *everyone*. It certainly got popular in a hurry. The four of us were the only ones who didn't have a bottle of it; even Mr. Simmons had two bottles on his desk.

"Alright, everyone. Let's get started," Mr. Simmons said as he pulled the overhead down and turned off the lights.

I heard several gulping sounds all around me. Everyone was slurping on their Wacky Water as Mr. Simmons talked. It was a little nauseating…but that might've been because of the cold.

Mr. Simmons took a swig of his bottle before starting up the PowerPoint. "Alright, so let's continue our discussion about World War II. Can someone tell me what propaganda is?"

I sniffled. I really had to sneeze. I was trying to hold it in with every ounce of my strength.

James raised his hand.

"Yes, Mr. Stump?" Mr. Simmons said, nodding to him.

James recited the definition, probably directly from the textbook or a dictionary. "The classic definition of the word is a collection of ideas, facts, or allegations spread deliberately to further one's—"

I couldn't hold it in anymore… "*Achoo!*" The entire room froze, all except for me, James, Nick and Kelly.

James didn't seem to notice, because he continued talking. "—cause, or to damage an opposing—"

"J-Man, he can't hear you," Nick said, pointing at Mr. Simmons. "He's all froze up."

James squinted toward Mr. Simmons. "Hmm, how irksome. That was the perfect definition, and I don't know where to begin again once they unfreeze."

I banged my fists on my desk. "Now do you guys understand my frustrations? Luckily, every time I Freeze-Frame the room, it doesn't last as long as before."

The room unfroze. A few seconds passed, and Mr. Simmons was still looking at James. "Continue, Mr. Stump," he said.

He looked at Mr. Simmons. "Right, uh, where was I?"

"Allegations to further one's what?"

"Ah, quite," James answered. "To further one's cause, or to damage an opposing cause. It was a practice that was used on both sides during the second World War, and was a means of demonizing the enemy while exalting one's own nation and or ideals. It was used to evoke feelings of fierce patriotism, but it was also used to justify evil-doings."

Mr. Simmons nodded. "What kind of evil-doings are you referring to?"

James had a solemn look on his face. "The inhumane and vile atrocities of the Holocaust comes immediately to mind. Unfortunately, America had its own vices when it came to such propaganda… We had many Japanese-Americans held up in concentration camps, too, all the while trying to convince ourselves that it was the correct thing to do."

Mr. Simmons pointed his finger at James. "Exactly right, that's where I was headed next. While propaganda can be used to promote positive patriotism, it can, and often does, have a dark side."

Mr. Simmons talked about propaganda for the rest of class, and he seemed to be pretty passionate about it. He talked about how all sides of the political spectrum have propaganda working for and against them, and that we should approach each issue and topic with a level head.

I was only half paying attention, though. I couldn't focus very much because I was trying to keep myself from sneezing to avoid Freeze-Framing the room again.

* * *

When the bell rang and school let out, all I heard from the other students was "Wacky Water this" and "Wacky Water that". Like…I really didn't get what the fuss was about. As we walked to the car, there were Wacky Water bottles in every trash can and recycling bin in the school parking lot, and several bottles littered the ground.

James looked down at one of the bottles. "If this Wacky Water business is truly the work of Doren's henchmen, this does not bode well. People seem to be addicted to the stuff, as you can see. Though, it's too early to substantiate such a claim. The evidence is circumstantial, but I have an inkling that something unseemly is going on at that bottling plant. It is highly suspicious. Though, I'd rather think with my brain than with my gastrointestinal system."

Nick slapped his stomach. "Hey, sometimes your gut feelings work better than your brain."

James looked at him and wrinkled his nose. "For you, maybe. These *gut feelings* seem to correlate well with those *road*—I mean—street smarts of yours. I seem to lack such street smarts, I'm afraid. I am much more comfortable when supplied with evidence to prove my suspicions."

"You *did* see the Ark in the factory, didn't you?" asked Kelly.

"I saw the Ark in *a* factory," James corrected. "But not necessarily that one."

I sighed. "But you saw how weird that Marina lady on the news acted, and look at the way everyone is downing this water like they're all stranded in the desert."

James put his hands in his pockets. "It is very suspicious, but we need more evidence. Let's see what they think at the organization."

As we drove to the Edania Organization, every channel on the radio was talking about Wacky Water and how it was taking the Force-Pointe Islands by storm, and the waterpark that was opening its doors tomorrow.

"If this is indeed the work of a Corrupted, then they are changing their pattern this time," said James, who was reading his biology textbook in the backseat.

"How so?" asked Kelly.

He closed his book. "Well, the first incident was just on Force-Pointe High's grounds, and the second was isolated to a section of Soraya Woods. This time, it involves all of the Force-Pointe Islands. I heard someone in English saying his cousin on Canaan Island bought out a local grocery store's supply yesterday. Even Paradise Island is selling it in bulk, or so I read during free period. This may suggest that the evil doers are becoming bolder, which is not good."

"Yeah, that means that we're gonna have to step up our game," said Nick, sounding more excited than worried.

We arrived at the Edania Organization and approached the front desk. The sweet older receptionist was working. Her name was Marge Lathem.

"Excuse me, Mrs. Lathem?" said Nick. He put his elbow on the desk, laid his chin on his hand and gave her a wide smile.

She looked up and laughed. "Oh, if it isn't my favorite group of young-uns. What can I do for you today?"

"We were wondering if we could talk to someone," he said politely. "Is Kristy in today? Or maybe G. or Dr. Steph?"

"You can talk to me," said a high-pitched voice.

We turned around and saw a petite girl standing behind us. She looked like a twelve-year-old who just got out of Sunday School. She wore a very formal bright blue dress, and her brown hair was pinned up in a fancy wavy pattern. Her face was fair and her cheeks were rosy. She looked like a living porcelain doll; the cute ones, not the creepy ones that look like they want to suck out your soul.

Nick knelt down to the girl's level. "Who are you, little girl?" He grinned at her. "You someone's daughter here?"

Mrs. Lathem gasped and hid her face under the desk.

The girl glared at Nick with eyes so angry, it looked like she was about to stab him in the neck with one of her hairpins. "Hmph, I'm not some little child. Don't speak to me in such a patronizing tone!"

Nick backed up. "Woah, woah, woah. Didn't mean to offend ya. Looks like someone needs a nap. Trust me, kid. You don't wanna grow up too fast."

She stomped her foot. "I'm eighteen, as a matter of fact. My name is Dr. Gabrielle, and I am one of the admins of the Edania Organization."

"You are?" he asked, his eyes widening in surprise. I was just as shocked as he was. She totally looked like she was twelve.

She took a deep breath. "Yes, I am the head of the weapons and ballistics department of the organization."

"Why are you dressed like a princess, then?" Nick asked. She grumbled and kicked him in the shin. "Ouch! What was that for?" he yelped, grabbing his leg and hopping up and down.

She fixed a strand of hair that had gone out of place. "That's for being rude! Do you talk to everyone this way? I'm dressed like this because I just returned from a conference in Tel Aviv. I was the keynote speaker."

"Sorry," said Nick, still hopping up and down.

She sighed. "Just make sure it doesn't happen again…" Her voice became more relaxed. "Anyway, I guess it's nice to finally meet our newest agents." She looked at Nick and rolled her eyes. "At least three of you. Please follow me. We can talk in my office. It will be more private."

Dr. Gabrielle started to walk toward the elevators.

"It's great to have you back, Dr. Gabrielle." said Mrs. Lathem.

Dr. Gabrielle stopped and faced the reception desk, which was just a little bit taller than she was. "It's nice to be back, Marge. I hope you and the family are doing well," she said warmly, completely changing her mood.

We started to follow her to the elevators.

Mrs. Lathem grabbed Nick's arm. "Please don't be too upset with her. She took her father's post as admin when he died a couple of months ago. She has a lot on her plate right now. She started college at a very young age and recently graduated with her doctorate. She's very brilliant, but knows very little as far as social interaction is concerned. You're lucky—last time someone said something to her about her age and size, she dropkicked them through a window. She's quite strong, given her petite appearance. But she's a sweet woman…once you get to know her."

"I'm waiting!" Dr. Gabrielle yelled impatiently. Yeah. Real sweet.

We ran to the elevators.

"So, how have your missions been going?" Dr. Gabrielle asked as we walked into the elevator.

"They've been…going alright," said Kelly, who was fidgeting with her hair, messing up her bun.

"What exactly is that supposed to mean?" she asked with a snooty tone.

James fiddled with his glasses. "For our first mission, we were disorganized to the point of being embarrassing, but we managed to acquire the first Ark. For our second, we managed to best two powerful Corrupted, but we lost the Ark and almost lost our lives in the process."

"Yes, I received word about that little fiasco of yours in Soraya Woods," she said in an undermining voice.

James twiddled his thumbs. "None of us are proud of it."

She looked at James and smiled. "Oh, don't worry so much about it." Her tone completely changed to being warm and comforting. "Oftentimes we learn more from our failures than from our successes. I'm sure the four of you have a bright future here."

We reached the third floor and followed Dr. Gabrielle down a long hall.

At the very end of the hall was a door that looked like it was made of bullet-proof glass. There was a small computer screen just to the left of the door, at Gabrielle's eye level…which wasn't that far off the floor. She entered a code.

*"Now scanning for corneal recognition,"* the Edania Organization's computer said. The computer screen scanned her eye. *"Welcome back, Dr. Gabrielle."*

The door slid open and she motioned us to follow her in. The room was spotless, very different from Gideon's disaster of an office. There was a tiny little office desk and chair in the corner of the room that looked like were from a toy store.

Dr. Gabrielle sat in the chair and looked at us sternly. "Now, do you have anything to report?"

"Yes," James said. "My Scan ability has shown me the next Ark."

"Really?" she said, folding her hands on her desk professionally. "What can you tell me about it?"

He looked down at the floor, discouraged. "Well, I…have a theory as to where it is, but I am afraid it cannot be substantiated with such minimal evidence."

"Where do you think it is?" she asked.

He didn't answer.

"He, I mean, *we* think it's at this water bottling plant that since recently has been abandoned." said Kelly, coming to James' rescue.

"An abandoned water factory? What makes you think that?" asked Dr. Gabrielle. She was hard to take seriously. Although she was acting totally professional, she looked like an elementary school kid sitting at their play table.

"Have you heard of Wacky Water?" asked Kelly.

"I can't say that I have," Dr. Gabrielle answered.

"It's this recent craze around the islands," Kelly said.

"Yeah, and the lady who runs the place was actin' pretty wacky herself," said Nick, making the cuckoo gesture with his finger.

Dr. Gabrielle looked at him with a very unamused face.

He stopped wiggling his finger around and straightened his posture. "Yeah, and everyone seems to be kinda addicted to the stuff."

Dr. Gabrielle was typing on her little computer. "Hmm—"

"It's also worth mentioning that they are opening a waterpark on the old factory's grounds," said Kelly. "But we were around that area just a little while ago for our last mission, and there was no sign of construction or anything. It's almost like it appeared overnight."

"James, is there anything else?" Dr. Gabrielle asked.

"I, uh…I do not wish to speculate," he said nervously.

She leaned back in her chair. "Oftentimes science and technology are advanced by what starts as speculation."

His face turned red and he nodded. "Well…this waterpark popping out of nowhere reminds me of Thistle's power in a way. She's one of the villains we bested on our last mission. She was able to create a hotel from a shapeshifting tree."

"Do you think this Thistle is somehow responsible?" the doctor inquired.

He shook his head. "No, it couldn't possibly be her. She was destroyed along with her Illusion Tree. Thistle controlled plants, and I am sensing a water-themed Dark-Segol here, if there is such a thing. But it seems very similar to Thistle's power. Again, this is all speculation. It's a feeling I have in my gastrointestinal system."

She raised her eyebrow. "Excuse me?"

"He has a gut feeling," Nick translated.

"Ah, I see." Dr. Gabrielle continued to type on the computer. "Well, it looks like your gut feeling may have some merit." She turned her computer screen toward us.

There was a map of Tolles Island on the computer screen, and the top quarter of it was bleeping green.

"What's that mean, doc?" asked Nick, squinting at the computer.

"There is a strong reading of Edaniite in the green area." She pointed. "However, there's powerful interference blocking its signal, so the program is having a hard time pinpointing the exact location. This bottling plant is the one in Soraya Woods, I assume? That factory is within the green area. So, it is possible this is where the Ark is. And there's only one Ark whose Edaniite barrier is strong enough to penetrate such strong interference."

"Which one is it?" I asked, without really wanting to know.

"I'd say it's Jordan's Ark," she answered, smiling at me. "You and Jordan have something in common, Abigail."

I looked at her, confused.

She laughed. "She was the only other agent to have the power of temporal immobilization. Well…at least this form of it."

"Tempra—huh?" asked Nick, puzzled.

"She could freeze time, too," I translated.

"Precisely," said Dr. Garbielle. "That means that if you get your hands on this Ark—"

"Does that mean I'd finally be able to control my Segol and not Freeze-Frame the room every time I panic or sneeze?" I blurted out.

Dr. Gabrielle nodded. "It should, yes. It'll also give your ability a power boost along with better control."

I turned around to walk out of the room. "Alright, let's get going, then!"

"Wait, I am still not entirely convinced that the bottling plant is where the Ark is being housed," said James.

"There's only one way to find out," I said. "Let's go check it out!" I could not believe what I was saying.

"Go," said Dr. Gabrielle.

James slumped his shoulders. "B-but—"

"There is compelling enough evidence to warrant an investigation," said Dr. Gabrielle. "Go to this waterpark and have a look around."

James put his head down. "I don't know…"

Dr. Gabrielle got out of her seat. "That's an order, James. Go tomorrow afternoon when the park opens. Be sure not to attract attention to yourselves, though. We have no idea what we're dealing with here if this place truly is under the control of a Corrupted. Whatever this interference is, it's powerful enough to muddle the Ark's signal. So, be sure to gather information and report back here before doing anything else."

James shied away. Nick put his arm around him and started dragging him out of the room. "C'mon, J-Man. You gotta be on your A-game! We need that big brain of yours."

James didn't answer; he just looked at Nick and smiled thinly.

"Alright, let's get this show on the road," I said as I practically ran out of the door to the elevator. Finally, I was going to have control over this stupid power of mine… We just needed to get that Ark before the bad guys did.

# CHAPTER 3: WATERPARK RECON—ABBY

"You've never been this optimistic about going on a mission, Abbs. What's the deal?" Nick asked, looking at me suspiciously. "We usually have to drag you with us kicking and screaming."

"Um, exaggerate much?" I said. "You've never had to drag me, I just never had much motivation to throw myself into mortal danger. Now I do. Getting my hands on that Ark will help get this crazy power of mine under control."

"I will say," James said, patting his bookbag, "having Marie's Ark in my possession has really helped with my Scan ability. The headaches are much less frequent, and I've even been able to activate it on my own a few times. Although keeping the Ark in my bookbag always makes me nervous, I don't want to lose it. But Gideon said he's working on something to remedy the issue, whatever that means."

I pointed at James. "See? He understands. Let's get going. The sooner we get there the sooner we get that Ark!"

Kelly pointed at the clock. "Abby, it's only lunchtime. We still have a few hours 'til we can go."

I shrugged. "We can skip a few classes, right? It's for the safety of mankind."

James gasped. "That cold of yours must have made you delirious if you think I am going to skip any class to go to a waterpark. If we skip school now, it won't be long until we're acting like a bunch of delinquents, doing things like littering or jay-walking."

"Don't get too crazy, J-Man," said Nick sarcastically.

I felt so full of energy, even though I had a cold. I *really* wanted to get my hands on that Ark. "Come on, guys. Can we please go now?"

Nick furrowed his eyebrows. "Would you be this excited if it was anyone else's Ark?"

I was insulted. "Of course I would…" I thought about it for a moment. "Well, maybe not. I'm sorry, I just want to be able to control my power, is that too much to ask?"

Nick nodded, like he really understood. "I get what you're saying, sis. You've had the hardest time out of all of us learning to control your superpower. Although, mine still goes a little crazy sometimes. Just the other day I accidentally burned my favorite pair of gym shorts up."

I crossed my arms. "That's because they were still wet because you forgot to turn the dryer on and you tried to dry it with your fire."

He put his head down. "It was still a tragic moment."

"Whatever, Nick," I said, rolling my eyes. "I really don't think you get it."

Kelly put her hand on my shoulder. "I know what you're going through. I mean, I seem to have my gravity power more or less under control, but this new electrical power is a different story. I've accidentally caused a power outage in my house at least four times."

"You have?" asked James, sounding more interested than sympathetic.

She nodded.

"Fascinating…" he said.

"Annoying is more like it!" she said.

The bell rang.

"Welp, I guess we'll finish this interesting conversation later," said Nick.

***

Every student and faculty member had bottles upon bottles of Wacky Water with them. In history class one kid, Greg Deer, had five bottles already empty, and four others on his desk.

"Woah there, Greg, think you got enough water?" asked Nick, tapping one of the bottles.

Greg took a large gulp of Wacky Water. "This stuff is delicious! And I gotta keep hydrated, I started feeling kind of sick last night. This stuff is supposed to help a lot."

He was kind of pale, and his eyelids looked a little heavy. I totally knew how he felt.

"How much of this Wacky Water did you consume since yesterday?" James asked, staring at the bottle.

He shrugged. "I dunno, ten or twelve?"

James looked at him like he was some kind of test subject. "Have you eaten anything?"

Greg shook his head. "Nope, haven't really had an appetite. Just super thirsty for Wacky Water."

James looked at the bottle more closely. "Hmm…"

"Okay, everyone, it's time to get started," Mr. Simmons said as he rushed into class. He had three bottles of Wacky Water with him. He looked a little frazzled. His hair was a mess, and his face looked pale, like he was getting sick, too.

On top of that, he struggled to teach. He looked more exhausted as class dragged on, and he finished two bottles of Wacky Water in five minutes or so. When the bell rang, he ran to his desk and grabbed his suitcase.

He huffed as he addressed the class. "Okay, that's it for today. No homework tonight so you guys can enjoy the afternoon at Wacky Water

World. I'm heading there myself with the wife and kids." With that, he rushed out of the door before any of us. Everyone else stampeded out of the room right behind him.

I looked around at the empty room. "What was that all about?"

"I dunno, but everyone practically ran each other over to get out of here…all to go to a waterpark?" said Nick.

"I've got a bad feeling about this," said Kelly.

James was muttering something to himself.

"Do you have something to share, James?" Kelly asked him.

He looked up at her. "Hmm?"

She gave him her typical disapproving look whenever he got super weird. "What are you muttering over there?"

He fixed his glasses. "Nothing. It's just that everyone's behavior is strange today. And look at how much Wacky Water they were drinking. Greg had several bottles, and when have you ever seen him consume anything other than energy drinks? He also looked sickly, more so than you, Abby. So did Mr. Simmons and a few other students. And it just so happens to be the people who had the most Wacky Water, like it's the water itself that is making them tired."

Kelly started nervously playing with her hair. "You think the water is somehow draining their energy like the Shadow Mantis or the Illusion Tree?"

He frowned. "It would seem that way, but I do not want to—"

"Jump to conclusions?" the three of us said in unison.

He glared at us. "Indeed."

"Well, let's head to that waterpark and check things out," Nick suggested. For once, I totally agreed.

***

We drove to the Edania Organization to let Dr. Gabrielle know that we were heading to Wacky Water World, and to change into our swimwear. I had a totally cute purple swimsuit with white floral imprints and matching flip-flops. Kelly had a gorgeous royal blue swimdress that looked like it was made for prom under the sea. Her shoes were totally gorgeous, too. They were high-heeled flip-flops, but not the tacky kind you get at the dollar store; they looked like what a princess would wear at a beach wedding.

We walked out of the dressing room and waited for the boys.

"What's taking them so long?" asked Kelly, looking at her phone.

"No clue," I said, tapping my foot. "But Nick always gives me crap about taking too long to get dressed. I mean, we're going to a waterpark, for goodness sake, it's not like he's dressing up."

Nick finally walked out of the dressing room. He was wearing his American flag swim trunks, a gray tank top, his ninety-dollar flip-flops he got from the sports clothing store, and a pair of sunglasses that were even more expensive than that. I swear, he would spend more money than me on clothes and accessories sometimes.

He was typing something on his phone as he walked. Not looking where he was going, he ran into Kelly and dropped his phone.

He and Kelly both bent down to pick it up, their heads bumped into each other, and it knocked his sunglasses off. She grabbed his phone and glasses and handed them to him.

Nick laughed as he stood up. "Sorry about that, Ms. Kell—" He looked up at her, and his eyes widened. "Wow."

Her face turned red. "Wow…what?" She touched her cheek. "Do I have something on my face?"

His face got redder than hers, which was saying something. "N-nothing," he stuttered. "It's just you look real nice. Suddenly I feel way underdressed."

"You look fine," she said, looking him up and down.

"Where's James?" I asked.

He pointed toward the changing room. "Still in there, but he sure is taking a while, isn't he?" He walked toward the dressing room. "J-Man, you alive in there?"

"I'm coming," he said, his voice muffled. He walked out of the dressing room, wearing a full-blown hazmat suit. "Alright, I'm ready to go," he said like it wasn't totally outlandish that he looked like he was on his way to a toxic waste dump.

Kelly stomped her foot. "You are *not* about to wear a hazmat suit to a waterpark!"

"Why not?" he protested.

She slapped her forehead. "We're supposed to blend in, first of all. Second, you're going to cause a panic. Third—" She looked him over again and threw her hands up in frustration. "Ugh, don't even get me started!"

James looked down in disappointment. "But…there are so many germs that could be lurking at that place."

Kelly marched toward him. "Take that thing off or so help me!"

He turned around to walk back into the dressing room, muttering to himself about microbes and pool water not having enough bleach.

As we waited for James to slip out of his hazmat suit, we were approached by Dr. Gabrielle. She was wearing a military uniform, and she looked like a little army dress-up doll. Of course, I didn't say that to her face. Although she was byte-sized, she was totally scary when she got mad.

"So, are you guys heading out?" she asked.

Nick saluted her. "Ma'am, yes, ma'am!"

"You look ridiculous saluting me wearing that, just so you know." She turned to me and Kelly. "Aww, you two look so cute!"

"Thank you," I said.

"I love your outfit too, doctor," said Kelly.

She looked down at her outfit and smiled. "Thanks. As the head of the weapon's engineering department, I've got to fit the part. But that doesn't mean I can't totally work the outfit!" She looked around the room with a puzzled expression. "Where's James?"

"Right here, Dr. Gabrielle," James answered as he walked out of the dressing room.

She turned around and took a step back in disgusted surprise. "Good glory, what are you wearing?"

James had on a turtleneck, heavy-duty cargo pants, a surgical mask, gloves, a hair net, and big old boots. "I figured they would all say that the hazmat suit was a bit much, so I brought these just in case they decided to be difficult. The turtleneck will protect my upper body, the pants will protect my lower body, the boots will protect my feet, and the mask and hairnet will protect my face and head against any pathogenic organisms that would dare come near me. Oh, and look." He pulled a can of something out of his bag. "It's the highest-grade disinfectant spray that I could get my hands on, so now I am ready to go to the microbial breeding ground that is this waterpark."

Dr. Gabrielle snatched the can of disinfectant from him. "You're supposed to blend in!" she screamed, shaking the can around. "You look like an idiot right now. Aren't you supposed to be the smart one? Don't tell me you're one of the Edania Organization's elite agents and have a bad case of OCD that you can't get under control? Ugh!" She stomped her foot like a child having a tantrum. She stopped after a moment and composed herself. "Ahem. At any rate, you *are* going to change out of that abomination of an outfit, right?"

"Must I?" he asked despairingly.

"If you wish to continue breathing," she said quickly.

He sighed. "But I have nothing else to change into, except for what I wore at school."

"That's better than—" she pointed up and down at his body "—this."

He sighed. "Very well." He walked back into the dressing room.

She watched James like a hawk as he walked into the dressing room, then she turned her attention to us. "Now that that's taken care of, I must remind you of something."

"What's that, doc?" asked Nick in his obnoxiously chipper voice.

She had a serious expression on her cute little face. "Remember that this is simply a reconnaissance mission. You are there just to gather information on our potential enemy. Do not engage said enemy until we know exactly who or what we're dealing with. Like I said before, if this is indeed a Corrupted, he or she is a powerful one. Once you've ascertained whether or not this *is* one of Doren's underlings, come back here and we will discuss a plan of action."

"You got it, Doctor Shortstuff!" said Nick, saluting her.

"Don't make me hurt you, Nicklaus," she rebuffed.

He gently slapped her shoulder. "I'm teasin'. C'mon, doc, have a sense of humor."

She sighed and rubbed her forehead like she was getting a migraine; a common reaction when talking to my brother. Then she smiled and let out a little chortle, another common reaction when talking to my brother. He can drive you absolutely nuts, but then he can turn around and make you laugh 'til you suffocate.

"I guess you're right…" she said softly. "I'm just not used to leaders of our teams being so laid-back and carefree. They're almost always walking around with scowls on their faces and speaking in grunts. I suppose I've forgotten to let loose and enjoy a joke once in a while since becoming an admin. Stephani has told me as much."

"Aww, she *does* know how to take a joke," Nick teased. "How cute."

She grabbed him by his shirt and pulled him down to her eye level. "Don't overdo it, or I'll hurt you! Now take your team and head out. I expect a full report when you return tonight." She let go of his shirt.

He saluted her again. "You got it. I'll probably leave the reporting part to J-Man. You know he'll get all technical and make it sound super smart."

James walked back out of the dressing room with the outfit he had from school. It was his usual one: black lab pants and one of his goofy science-pun shirts and a lab coat. The shirt he was wearing had a picture of an animated microscope and under it, it said *Microbiologists take cellfies*. Apparently, he thought it was the funniest thing ever; it was his favorite one to wear.

"Dear Lord in heaven," said Dr. Gabrielle, looking at James with disdain. "This…is what you actually wear to school?"

"What's wrong with it?" James asked.

She looked at Kelly, her eyebrows raised. "Is he serious?" she asked. Kelly nodded sympathetically, and Dr. Gabrielle looked back at James. "Like I said, you're supposed to be inconspicuous. What you're wearing is the exact opposite."

"I refuse to wear anything different," he said in an annoyed tone.

"If James wore normal clothes, everyone from school would make a spectacle of it. That might bring unwanted attention to us," said Kelly.

The doc rolled her eyes. "Fine, just go. And make sure to report back by tonight so we can come up with a plan."

***

We left the Edania Organization and headed toward Wacky Water World. I didn't know what to expect as far as our mission was concerned. I mean, what if this wasn't a Corrupted incident and we go in guns-a-blazin' like Nick usually does and we make fools of ourselves and the organization? On the other hand, what if this was a Corrupted and we get attacked unawares because we were being too careful when we should have gone in guns-a-blazin'?

"What I'm wearing isn't that bad, is it?" asked James all self-conscious.

"You look fine, James," said Kelly, who was looking out the window.

I turned around and smiled at him. "Yeah, that outfit is totally you."

His head slumped down. "But Dr. Gabrielle acted like what I'm wearing is some sort of grievous sin as far as outfits are concerned. So, if this outfit is the totality of me, am I a grievous sin?"

"You're all good, bro," said Nick. "I happen to like your shirts with the sciency jokes, even though I don't understand most of 'em."

James felt his shirt. "I just don't do swimwear…I don't want to subject myself to all of the potentially nasty microbes that are crawling around that place. Not to mention, my exceedingly pale skin would blind everyone there. No, I prefer to keep my shirt on, thank you."

We reached Wacky Water World. James was right about its proximity to Soraya Woods. The trees from the thick woods towered over the right side of the park. He was also right about how noticeable its construction would have been. Some of the waterslides were bigger than the bottling factory itself, and we would definitely have noticed them being built when we ventured into the woods to take care of Thistle and Dr. Barbaas.

The parking lot was huge and decrepit. It looked like it had been abandoned for years. There were cracks everywhere with weeds growing out of them. But now the parking lot was packed so full that we had to park all the way in the back in a field next to the woods.

We got out of the car and headed toward the park's entrance.

"Woah, this place looks awesome!" said Nick, admiring the potentially evil waterpark. He was carrying a beach towel and his gym bag.

"Why are you taking all of that stuff with you?" James asked.

He tapped his gym bag. "We're supposed to blend in, right? Well, I'm bringing what everyone else would bring to a waterpark."

"We're not here to relax by the pool," I reminded him. "We're here to check things out and make sure nothing fishy is going on around here!"

"I know, I know," he said. "But I can still get my tan on while we're investigating, can't I? It's called multitasking, Abbs."

Kelly sighed. "I wish I could be as carefree as you are, especially since we might be walking behind enemy lines."

Nick put his arm around her, and her face reddened. "C'mon, Kelly. It's easy, just hang with me and you'll be as cool as a winter's day," he said as they started walking. I noticed Kelly wasn't complaining about the fact that his arm was still around her shoulder.

A vile squeal came from behind us. "Nicky, is that you?"

I turned around to see Alyssa sprinting in our direction. Nick looked in Alyssa's direction, and Kelly slipped out of his grip.

Alyssa slipped between Kelly and Nick, and knocked Kelly on the ground with her totally bony butt.

"Oops, how clumsy of me. Sorry, Kelly," said Alyssa in the fakest sweet voice I'd ever heard. "Anyway, Nicky, promise you'll go down a water slide with—"

Nick, apparently ignoring her, bent down and helped Kelly up. "You okay?"

"Yeah, I'm fine," she mumbled, brushing herself off.

Alyssa squeezed in between both of them again. "You heard her, she's fine. Now, promise me you'll go on one of the slides with me?"

He looked at her with a neutral expression. "Uh, sure," he said.

"Great, see you inside," Alyssa squealed as she flicked her reddish hair in Kelly's face.

"She sure is friendly," he said, watching her walk away.

Kelly grunted. "To you, maybe…" she said as she started walking toward the entrance without us.

"Well, now you went and did it," I told Nick, then I ran up to Kelly.

"What did I do?" I heard Nick ask James.

I caught up to her "You alright, Kelly?"

"I'm fine," she said in her high-pitched lying voice.

I watched angrily as Alyssa walked into a large crowd of people waiting to get into the park. "I don't know who that witch thinks she is, pushing you and clinging all over my brother like that."

She crossed her arms. "Well, he seems to enjoy the attention, not that it's any of my business."

"Oh, Kelly," I said with a sigh. "You've got to know something about Nick. He's oblivious to any sort of flirtation, even when it's blatantly obvious. He doesn't realize that the dumb peacock is flirting. He just thinks she's trying to be nice."

"Oh, she's being nice, alright…" she muttered.

I smiled at her. "Trust me, she's not his type."

She glanced over at me, without even managing a fake smile. "Like I said, it's none of my business."

We ran into the giant crowd of people waiting in line to get into the park. Everyone else in line had at least two bottles of Wacky Water in their hands.

"Woah, this place is packin'," said Nick as he and James caught up to us.

James started to breathe heavily. "So…many…people. So…many…germs!"

There was a giant TV screen above the main entrance to the park that turned on. That Marina woman came on and addressed the crowd of people.

"Welcome to Wacky Water World!" Her voice was cheerful and pleasant. "I hope you'll enjoy all of the fun and exciting attractions we have here. We have a children's play area, a lazy river that encamps the entire property, a wave pool, and several thrilling waterslides. And that's just the outside of the park! Inside, you'll find Wacky William's theater, where you'll meet the fun-loving jester himself as he uses his wits to fight a terrible water dragon to save the beautiful Princess Waterdrop. You'll also find our indoor waterslide, the Tunnel of Love, that twists and turns both inside of the building and out, ending up in a giant luxury swimming pool on the factory's lower floor."

"She sounds way too happy," I said, looking up at the screen. "She's probably evil."

"She does give off a creepy vibe," said Kelly.

Marina continued. "Now remember, the actual manufacturing part of the plant is off limits. There is absolutely no entry allowed." Her sapphire eyes suddenly became cold, and a creepy grin crept on her face. "We would hate for there to be an accident for any of our dear visitors here. That would indeed be a tragedy."

Marina's face went back to being serene and graceful. "Now, enjoy your time here at Wacky Water World, and make sure you visit all of our attractions. Get in there and have fun!"

The front gates opened, and everyone trampled over each other to get in.

We were the last ones to enter the park, but we did that on purpose so we wouldn't get stampeded.

"Woah," Nick said in amazement. "This place is sweet! Too bad it might be evil, or I'd definitely come here all the time."

James looked around, repulsed. "You would have to come here without me. I can practically feel all of the microorganisms crawling on me." He cringed. "Too many people…not enough bleach."

"So, where should we look first?" Kelly asked, probably to stop James from going into freakout mode.

"Th-the most likely place to find any clues would be i-in the factor-y," said James with a stutter. Guess he was already in freakout mode. He was trembling like a chihuahua.

"What is the matter with you, James?" asked Kelly.

He looked at her, his face paler than usual. "Th-is place is m-making me so very anxious… I am trying not to have a p-panic attack. I need to stay focused on our—eek!" He practically leaped out of his skin when a little kid sneezed on his leg. "C-can we please get this over with?" he said as he pulled some disinfectant spray out of his bookbag and sprayed his pantleg.

We headed toward the indoor part of Wacky Water World, which was an extension of the bottling factory. We walked around one of the large pools to get to the building.

"Nickyyyy!" Alyssa yelled from several yards away. *Oh, God.*

She and her loyal peacocks congregated around Nick. "Hey, Nicky. How do you like it here so far?" Alyssa asked.

He smiled at her. "It's pretty cool. There's a lot of stuff to do around here."

Her eyes fluttered. "Well, you know, there's an indoor waterslide called the Tunnel of Love, and they say that if two people ride together for their first time, they're meant to be."

"Excuse us," Kelly interrupted. "We're actually busy right now."

Alyssa grabbed Nick's arm and rubbed all over it with her hand. "Wow, you sure have strong arms."

"Thanks," he said. "I do a lot of heavy lifting."

Kelly grunted quietly and clenched her fists. There was a loud scraping noise coming toward us. A beach chair behind Alyssa was moving by itself, surrounded by a purple glow. It screeched as it dragged forward, picking up speed as it approached. The chair swept Alyssa off of her feet and drove her into the pool.

"Oh, no. What a shame," said Kelly with absolutely no empathy as she grabbed Nick and started walking toward the factory. "I feel *so* bad for the chair."

"You think she's gonna be okay?" he asked, looking back at the pool.

"She'll be fine. Her head's full of hot air, so there's no way she'll drown," she said.

James followed behind them. I took a moment to enjoy the sight of

Alyssa's totally flustered expression as she watched Kelly and my brother walk together into the building. That was a perfect moment. And the way Kelly angrily threw the chair at her with her superpower was even better. Who knew the girl could be so jealous? Luckily, nobody had seemed to notice that the chair was glowing purple.

"Abbs!" Nick yelled.

I snapped out of my feeling of euphoria and joined the rest of the group.

# CHAPTER 4: TUNNEL OF LOVE—KELLY

We entered the indoor area of the park, which connected to the bottling plant.

"Kelly, your nails are kinda digging into my arm," said Nick, wincing.

I let go of his arm. "Sorry." But was I?

He rubbed his arm. "What was that all about, anyway?"

"We're on a mission. We aren't here to socialize," I said in a snippier tone than I intended.

"Yes, ma'am," he said. He grinned at me. "Just promise you won't hit me and I'll do whatever you say. Maybe they should'a chosen you to be the leader."

"Shut up," I said, trying not to smile. I didn't know why I got so upset every time Alyssa and her peacocks threw themselves all over him; it's not like I was jealous or anything. What a silly thought.

James and Abby walked in behind us.

"This place is huge," said Abby, looking around. "It's crazy that they could fit so much in here."

She wasn't kidding. I looked at the illuminated map of the indoor part of the park. There was a water coaster over to the right of the entrance, a theater to the left, and the Tunnel of Love was up the set of stairs straight ahead.

*Tunnel of love…that's the stupid ride Alyssa wanted to go on with Nick. What a tacky name*, I thought as I looked straight ahead at the entryway to the slide.

"Where should we start looking, J-Man?" Nick asked.

James seemed to have calmed down a little bit. He walked up to the map and examined it closely. "Hmm, hard to say. I could not tell if the Ark was in a higher or lower area with Scan. I suppose we just start looking, and if we start to feel the Ark's pull, we will know we're close. All I know is that it was in a room with water vats and pipes, so it's safe to assume that if it is here, it's in the actual factory area. We just need to find a way into the plant itself."

Nick pointed over toward a sign that said *Theater*. "That's the closest place. Let's start there."

We rented a few lockers and put our stuff in them, then headed to the theater.

The theater was up a small flight of stairs that had red carpet laid over it. It definitely was not what I expected. I thought we were going to walk into an obnoxiously animated theater with tacky streamers and goofy music playing in the background. But it was decorated beautifully. The outside looked like the Chinese Theatre in Hollywood, but much smaller. Inside, it looked just like one of those old-time theaters, the ones that you would have to dress up to go to. There was one auditorium that you could enter from a door to the left or right, or up a large staircase, where a golden chandelier was hanging from the ceiling above it.

There were too many people packed around the doors on the main floor, so we went up the stairs and walked into the auditorium. It was dark, but you could tell it was a full house. There was commotion everywhere, and I could just make out the shadows of people moving all around us.

A musical chime sounded to let everyone know it was showtime. A spotlight focused on the ceiling, where something was being lowered from the catwalk. Whatever it was, it was so big that it was connected to four thick wires.

Abby gasped. "Nope, nope, absolutely not! I am *so* out of here!"

She was screaming about the giant caricatured animatronic jester's head that lowered onto center stage. It had a psychotically happy smile and big bulging round eyes that seemed to stare right at you no matter where you were in the theater. I wasn't scared of clowns, but this thing gave me the creeps.

"What's wrong, Abbs?" Nick asked as he poked her side. "Is the clown thing freakin' you out or something?"

She slapped his hand. "You know it is! I *hate* clowns, they're creepy and evil!" she cried as she backed away toward the door.

"I believe that technically it would be categorized as a jester, not a clown," said James.

"Close enough," Abby said shakily. "Can we please get out of here?"

The animatronic jester's head started to talk. Its lower mandible moved up and down as it did. "Ladies and gentlemen, boys and girls, welcome to Wacky William's theater!" it said in a very theatric and excitable voice. "In just a moment, you will be immersed into my world as I attempt to slay the fierce sea dragon to save the lovely Princess Waterdrop. Please take your seats and turn off those phones until intermission. And thank you for coming to Wacky Water World!"

The animatronic head started to ascend, and the curtain opened to reveal some really bizarre scenery. The background had carved-out blue mountains with water gushing out of them like hydro-volcanoes. A terrible screech came from above us, and an animatronic monster zigzagged above the audience. It looked like one of those serpentine dragons you see at a Chinese New Year celebration. It was deep blue with green spikes that ran along its spine. As it slithered in the air, it sprayed mist all over the place. When the mist touched my arms, they started to tingle a little...as though they were falling asleep.

A jester popped up out of nowhere on stage. His face was identical to the mechanical head: sheet white with red cheeks and hooked nose, eyes large and exaggerated, and a psychotically happy smile. I sympathized with Abby…this guy was creepy.

"I, Wacky William, will slay thee, oh demon of the seas!" he yelled overdramatically. He jumped off stage and started chasing the dragon around the auditorium.

Abby kept her hand on the door. "Ugh, I hope the dragon eats Wacky William. That would be the best ending for this play."

"That was kind of dark, Abby," I said.

"Yeah well, life's full of dark things, Kelly," she answered. "Now can we please get out of here before I have a panic attack?"

James nodded. "I concur. I am not feeling the pull from the Ark here, anyway. And it's unlikely that the entrance to the factory section is behind the stage."

The dragon flew right above us, and Wacky William started running up the stairs after it.

Abby was practically out of the room already. "I really wish I could freeze the room right now!" she squeaked right before the door shut behind her.

The rest of us joined her outside of the auditorium.

"Why are you so freaked out about clowns?" I asked her.

Nick chuckled. "At our sixth birthday party a clown did the sawing-in-half trick and our stepdad was the lucky volunteer, and it freaked her out. She wouldn't calm down even after she realized that our stepdad was in one piece."

Abby shivered. "That's not all of it. The clown tried to cheer me up with balloon animals, and he chased me around the yard trying to make me one. His high-pitched voice and white face and red nose and bloodthirsty eyes, it was terrible. And now I hate clowns!"

"I find them to be rather unnerving as well," said James. "They are always so happy… Nobody is that happy all of the time unless they have psychopathic tendencies."

"Well, that was a waste of time," I said. "Where should we look next?"

"Hmm, we could walk up the stairs to the Tunnel of Love," James suggested.

"Can we go somewhere else first, please?" I asked, thinking about Alyssa.

James pointed toward the slide's entrance as we walked out of the theater. "I have been thinking, based on the building's construct and the location of rides and such, I believe that there may be an entrance to the factory somewhere up there."

"Why can't we just go around back and sneak in that way?" I asked, really not wanting to go up there.

He raised his eyebrow. "We are supposed to be inconspicuous. If we go into an unauthorized zone, we would certainly be noticed. We're just going up there to see if there is a possible entrance to the factory."

Nick looked at me with his eyebrows furrowed. "Why don't you want to go up there?"

I looked away from him. "I—I just don't."

"Well, I don't wish to be here at all…" James said begrudgingly. "But, it's our mission."

It looked like it was impossible to avoid. "Fine, a quick look," I relented.

Nick sprinted up the stairs, and James followed after him.

Abby stopped me from walking up the stairs. "So," she said. "What's the *actual* reason you don't want to go up there?"

I looked at her, trying to keep my facial expression under control. "There doesn't have to be a reason. I just don't."

"Is it because of Alyssa?" she asked.

My jaw dropped. "Of…of course not! Don't be crazy, let's go!"

We walked up the white-and-black checker-tiled stairs. The staircase spiraled up, and the climb was pretty high. Narrow, too. The walls made it a little too snug for my liking. Luckily, the line was surprisingly small when we got up to the top.

The waterslide was one of those giant ones that sent two-person tubes through it. There was a decorative sign above the entrance to the slide that had *Tunnel of Love* slapped across it in purple and pink colors.

"Do you feel the pull?" James asked suddenly.

I jumped a little. "Wh-what pull?"

"Yeah, I do," said Nick, nodding.

"It feels like it did before," Abby said excitedly. "It's totally the Ark."

Oh, that pull. I closed my eyes and concentrated. There was no mistaking it; it was the pull of the Ark. It was as though an unseen force was trying to pull me toward a door at the other end of the room.

"Abby, can you Freeze-Frame the room?" James asked.

"I'll try," she said doubtfully.

"Next!" one of the guys who ran the slide yelled. Both men who worked the slide looked like bodybuilders who could pick up a house with one hand. The other guy plopped a couple into a tube and pushed them down the slide.

We were the next ones in line. Abby took a deep breath and flicked her hands out, and the room went completely still. Even the water jets on the slide were immobilized.

"Nice goin', Abbs!" said Nick, admiring her handiwork.

She sighed. "I'm just surprised I was able to do it because of how my ability has been acting up lately."

James walked toward the door. "Although time is frozen here, I can still feel the Ark's pull coming from the other side of this door."

Nick followed him. "Alright, then that settles it, the Ark is definitely here somewhere."

I started to make my way to the door, too, but the room unfroze before I could make it.

"Hey, you can't go over there!" one of the bodybuilders yelled. He grabbed my arm. "Time to go down the tunnel, little girl."

Nick ran over and grabbed his arm and freed me from his grasp. "Watch it, buddy!"

"Calm down, kid," said the man as he grabbed Nick too. "I'm just going to guide you two to the ride."

"B-but—" I said as we got closer to the slide.

He plopped me in the front of the tube, then dropped Nick right behind me.

The man smiled creepily at me. "Now, girly. Lean back a little and hold on tight. This slide can get pretty fast."

I looked up at him. "But I don't want to—"

The man laughed. "Relax little girl, I'm sure your boyfriend'll hold you nice and safe-like."

My ears felt hot. "He's not, I m-mean we're not, it's not like we—"

The man pushed our tube forward and we started to tilt downhill. I almost fell out of the tube, but Nick pulled me back and I leaned into him. "I got'cha, Ms. Kelly. I won't let you fall out," he said as he smiled at me.

I could feel the heat in my ears spread to my face. I really hoped I wasn't blushing as much as I thought I was.

We flew down the steep decline. Nick held me tight as we raced down. His strong arms were firm and sturdy, and I knew I was secure…and he was actually pretty comfortable to lean on. Not that I'd ever admit such a thing.

The slide turned a corner and we came to a sudden stop. It was pitch black, and I couldn't see a thing.

A voice came over a loudspeaker right above us. It sounded like that Marina woman. "Please stay inside the tube until the end. You will be making a few stops on your descent down the Tunnel of Love. Your first stop is the beautiful Princess Waterdrop's throne room, where you'll get to meet Her

Highness in person."

We started going a little faster until we reached a large room. The slide track looped around a large, circular platform. Eerie music that sounded like it came from a xylophone played in the background. Our tube entered a roundabout, and we slowly drifted along the platform. There was a life-sized animatronic doll wearing an aquamarine dress sitting on a coral throne on the stage. Its face looked like a porcelain doll's, and it had long brown hair. The doll stood up and waved its hand at us as we slowly moved forward.

"Hello," it said in a recorded female's voice. It sounded a little crackly, like its speaker was slightly broken. "I am Princess Waterdrop. I am so very pleased to meet you."

Its face was unnerving, especially its big, round eyes. I could hardly stand looking at it. I never liked porcelain dolls.

Nick held me closer to him. "That thing's creepy, isn't it?" he said, apparently reading my mind.

We finally made it to the other side of the room and shot down another steep drop. We turned another corner, and we were outside for a moment. The slide's tubing was see-through, so we could see outside perfectly. It was a pretty nice view of the park and the woods beyond it, until we dropped back down into the dark. We reached another room with a circular platform. Carousel music was playing in the background, and the room looked like a giant red-and-yellow striped tent. In the center of the room was an animatronic doll of Wacky William, and it was dancing all around the platform.

"Hope you're having tons of fun, fun, fun with your significant other in the Tunnel of Love," it said in an animated voice. "And now that you've ridden this magical slide, it means that you'll live happily ever after one day!"

My face felt hot again. *Why am I blushing? It's not like we're dating or anything, so it doesn't count. It's just a stupid ride, anyway.*

"Boy, I hope they don't make Abbs ride this… She's not gonna like this part." Nick chuckled.

"Huh?" I said, snapping out of my thoughts. "Oh, yeah, because she hates clowns."

Wacky William continued as we reached the end of the loop. "Hope you like the final plunge—of looove!"

*Shut it, you stupid clown!*

We plummeted downward into the darkness, took another sharp turn, and I could see the light below. We skimmed through the water as we flew out of the end of the slide. We stopped suddenly, and we both fell out of the tube. We were in a sectioned-off corner of a giant pool. It looked like it covered the entire area of the building's lower level. There weren't very many people in the pool, even though it looked like it could fit a thousand people.

Nick waded toward the pool rope that sectioned the water slide exit from the rest of the pool and lifted it up for me. His tank top stuck to his skin, and I could see just how muscular he was underneath. "That was…something," he said as I walked past the rope.

"Creepy is what it was," I said as I wrung my hair out. "And now my hair is soaked…great."

We heard a piercing scream, and Abby came flying through the slide's exit, and she was all by herself. She hopped out of her tube and walked toward us, shivering.

"That…was…one of the worst experiences of my life!" she said. "I may need therapy after that. I thought my tube was going to get stuck in that circus tent room."

"Why were you by yourself, Abbs?" Nick asked, holding the rope up for her, too.

"I dunno," she said in a snarky tone. "Guess that means I'm going to die alone."

Another tube came shooting out of the slide; it was James. He was also by himself. He slowly got out of the tube. He looked more freaked out than Abby. "I would very much like to go home now… I am all wet. They forced me on the slide. They wouldn't let me go back down the stairs. I was not even in proper swimwear!" He held his glasses up, and they were soaked. "And look at my glasses, just look!"

"Well, now that our mission's accomplished, we can go," I said.

We waded to the end of the pool and got out.

"Aw, man!" Nick yelled.

"What? Is it the jester thing?" Abby squealed as she frantically looked around.

He slapped the water in frustration. "I lost one of my flip-flops, and my sunglasses!"

"Huh," I said. "My shoes are still on."

We got out of the pool and Nick stomped his foot. "Those flip-flops were expensive, and so were those glasses! They must have come off on the slide. Let's go back and get 'em."

"No, we're not going back. Are you crazy?" Abby squeaked.

"If they got stuck on the slide, it is improbable that we would be able to find them," James said.

"That's what you get for spending so much on them and not keeping better tabs," said Abby.

Nick frowned and he looked behind her. "Hey, do you hear that? It kinda sounds like a clown's nose honking."

She cringed. "Shut up, Nick! Let's just get out of here, please?"

Nick sighed. "Fiiine."

We walked out of the pool area and down a strange, narrow hall. Red curtains lined the walls. At the very end of each wall, there were two windows. As we approached them, an animatronic doll of Princess Waterdrop popped up behind the window on the left side, and Wacky William popped up behind the window to the right. Abby practically tore Nick's shirt off she grabbed on to it so tightly, briefly revealing his lean, muscled stomach. I could feel a fresh, hot blush start to creep onto my face, so I looked away and hoped nobody noticed.

"Easy there, Abbs!" he yelled. "This is one of my favorite shirts!"

"Let's just get out of here, please…" she said, keeping her eyes closed.

We reached the main area on the inside of the park.

"Aw man, we're all soaked!" said Nick.

James took his glasses off and tried to clean them. "It *is* a waterpark, so one would expect to get wet…although I, for one, am not a fan of wearing wet clothes."

"At least the three of us have swimwear on, James," Abby said.

He sighed. "I had no idea that they would force me on a ride. Those rapscallions, I truly hope they're Corrupted so we can teach them a lesson…" He looked at Nick. "Go catch them on fire!" he said, and I couldn't tell if he was being serious.

Nick laughed. "That would be a little extreme, don'tcha think?"

"I suppose you're right…" James said as he put his glasses back on. "Let's make sure that they're evil, and then you can catch them on fire."

Nick raised his eyebrow. "What happened to 'you can't catch everything on fire to solve your problems, Nick'?"

"This is different," James said, crossing his arms. "Clearly."

"Nickyyy!" Alyssa's voice echoed through the entire building.

"Speaking of evil," Abby muttered.

Alyssa and her group of peacocks once again congregated around Nick.

Alyssa put her skanky palm on his chest. "Wow, Nicky, now that you're all wet, your shirt really shows off your muscles!"

Abby hacked. "Someone please kill me. Where's that Shadow Mantis when you need it?" she whispered to me.

Alyssa kept poking at his stomach. "So, are you ready to go on the Tunnel of Love with me?"

"Sorry, Alyssa, I just got off of it with Kelly," he said.

She took a step back. "Wh-waah? Why would you do something like that?"

He shrugged. "We kinda had to. We really weren't given a choice."

"Is that supposed to be some kind of predestination thing?" she asked angrily.

He looked at her, confused. "Pre—huh?"

"She is implying that you two were placed on the ride by some unseen, guiding force," said James.

"You lost me," Nick said to him.

James pointed at Alyssa. "Basically, the misguided and obviously envious Alyssa thinks that because you and Kelly went on the Tunnel of Love together…from the implications of the foolish saying about the fate of two people who ride it together for the first time, that somehow now you and Kelly are—"

"Leaving, we're leaving," I interrupted before he embarrassed me even more. "We have somewhere to be."

Abby grabbed James's arm. "Let's go, Mr. Overanalyze."

He followed her. "You can never overanalyze. Besides, such a fable about destiny being dictated by a waterslide is irrational."

I grabbed Nick and we started walking away from the peacocks. "Sorry, Alyssa. Guess you'll just have to find someone else to ride the Tunnel of Love with."

I heard her grunt and humph. What a perfect moment!

Nick and I reached the illuminated map in the center of the indoor area of the park.

"Why do you keep draggin' me away like I'm some sort of five-year-old?" Nick complained, then he gave me his cute but totally obnoxious grin. "If you wanna hold hands, just say so."

I let go of his arm. "D-don't be ridiculous! We have work to do, and we can't waste time on dealing with annoying classmates."

He chuckled. "Yes, ma'am. So, what's the plan?"

I turned my head away from him. "I don't know, you're the leader."

"Alright," he said. "Let's go back and tell Dr. Shortstuff that we know the Ark's here somewhere."

We joined Abby and James at our lockers.

"And that's why you need to think before you speak!" Abby said, lecturing James.

"I always think before I speak. I am not a simpleton," he said matter-of-factly.

She shook her head. "Apparently you are when it comes to social interaction."

"What's she yelling at you for, J-Man?" Nick asked.

James looked at Nick. "Because, I was going to say that you and Kelly are—"

Abby stepped on his foot.

"Ouch, that hurt!" he yelled.

"Oops, sorry, James," Abby said innocently.

Nick laughed. "Careful, man. Abby may act all innocent, but if you make her mad she'll whoop ya good."

James was hopping on one foot. "But I didn't do anything."

"You guys ready to head back to the organization?" Nick asked.

"Indeed," James said indignantly, hobbling on one foot. "We must fill Dr. Gabrielle in on our findings here."

Abby started walking. "Yeah, let's go. The sooner we get out of here, the sooner we can get that Ark. I also hope we can burn this place to the ground and get rid of that stupid clown—"

"Technically, he's a jester," James corrected.

"Technically, you have another foot I can stomp on," she snapped.

James fell back a few steps. "I apologize. Please don't hurt me."

Abby quickened her pace. "I just want this mission to be over with so I don't have to see that *jester* ever again, and I want to be able to not accidentally freeze entire rooms every time I sneeze or panic."

As we exited the park, there was a man dressed up as Wacky William pacing around the exit. As if he could smell her fear, he approached Abby. "Thank you for visiting Wacky Water World, come back soon!" he said in a very animated voice.

"Get away from me!" she yelled.

He got closer to her. "Aww, don't be so sad…"

She pointed her finger at him. "If you come one step closer to me, you'll get it!"

"I would listen to her," James warned. "She's scary."

Wacky William backed up.

Abby turned around and started powerwalking. "Ugh, I am so over this place!"

We walked back to the car, and Nick was trying not to step on the hot blacktop with his bare foot. "Ack!" he yelled as he started to hop. "I stepped on a rock!"

I looked at him and smiled. *He really is a goofball.*

"So," said Abby as she snuck up right next to me with a creepy grin on her face. "What'cha looking at?"

"Nothing," I answered. "Just walking."

She nodded. "Sure, sure. So, now that you two have ridden the Tunnel of Love together, when's the wedding?"

My face felt hot again…for the five hundredth time that day.

"Oh, c'mon," she said. "I'd love for you to be my sister-in-law."

"It didn't mean anything," I whispered. "It's just a stupid water ride. Besides, we were forced on, so it's not like it would have counted anyway."

She had a blank look on her face. "So, what you're saying is that you haven't planned the wedding?"

I sighed. "Abby, he's just a friend."

"You mean you don't like him?" she asked.

"Sure I do, but not like that," I answered.

She smiled wildly at me. "Then why is your face so red?"

"Sunburn," I said.

"Alright…" She seemed to relent. "But I think you two would make a good couple. And you can't argue with waterpark lore. It's always true, you know?"

"So that means you're going to be alone for the rest of your life?" I said, raising an eyebrow.

She put her hands up. "N-no! Obviously it didn't count for me!" she said, flustered. She sighed. "Fine, I'll stop. But you'd be a whole lot better for him than Alyssa."

We got to the car. Nick opened his trunk and got a pair of socks and shoes out and slipped them on. "Ah, so much better. Alright, you guys ready to go?"

Nick opened the door and set the seat back. After he tossed some towels on the seats, he bowed and motioned me into the car. "Your ride, milady."

I could hear Abby giggle from the passenger's seat.

I got into the car and buckled my seatbelt.

James hopped in right next to me. "Hey, Kelly. Why is your face so red? We weren't outside long enough to get a sunburn."

Abby tossed her purse at him and it hit him in the stomach.

"Ouch, what was that for?"

Nick hopped in and closed the door. "Alright, let's get back."

We rode back to the organization. I had high hopes that this would be a successful mission. I mean, we'd already found the approximate location of the Ark, and we really hadn't run into much trouble, unless you count Alyssa.

# CHAPTER 5: ROUGH WATERS AHEAD—KELLY

"You're sure the Ark is somewhere on Wacky Water World's premises, then?" Dr. Gabrielle asked. She was still wearing her little army uniform, and it felt like we were being interrogated by Military Barbie.

"Yes, we felt the unmistakable pull of the Ark," said James. "It is definitely somewhere in that facility."

Dr. Gabrielle nodded. "Did you sense any evil?"

Abby rolled her eyes. "Yeah, but not the kind that we can take care of."

Dr. Gabrielle looked at her with conviction in her eyes. "I wouldn't sell yourself short. I'm sure you can deal with whatever Corrupted comes against you—"

Abby snickered. "I wasn't talking about a Corrupted. This evil has her humanity intact…somewhere."

"Ah," Dr. Gabrielle said, nodding her head in understanding. "Perhaps I should've asked if you sensed any Corrupted activity?"

"We could not," James answered. "I tried using my Scan ability…but I was unsuccessful. Although, it may have been the stress of being in such an awful place." James's face went pale. "They made me go down that slide. I mean, I might as well have slid down a sewer pipe." He cringed.

Nick lit a fireball in his hand. "So, now that we know the Ark is there, should we burn the place down and grab it?"

Dr. Gabrielle glared at him. "You will do no such thing!"

Nick snuffed the fire out and shrugged. "I was just kidding, Dr. Shortstuff."

She sighed loudly and took off her hat. "This is no time for joking. This mission will require your full attention. It will require strategy. Now that we know the Ark is there, we can assume that the powerful force that our computer detected is indeed a Corrupted, and a very strong one at that."

Nick's expression got more serious. "Alright, have it your way. What's the plan?"

She seemed to ease up when she saw Nick was actually paying attention to her. "Allow me to do some research, and I will pass it along to James. He will form a plan to get into the water factory without being detected. Then you, Nicklaus, will come up with a plan to neutralize the Corrupted, should you run into them."

"Me?" Nick asked, pointing at himself.

She nodded stiffly "You *are* the leader of the group, correct?"

Nick squirmed in his seat. "Yeah, but that sounds like more of a J-Man thing."

She seemed to take notice of Nick's anxiety. She thought for a moment, then turned to James. "Are you comfortable coming up with a battle plan as well?"

James looked at Nick thoughtfully and shook his head. "I believe Nick should come up with the plan of battle, should it arise."

Nick looked at James, almost meekly, which was not an expression that normally crept onto his face. "But you're the smart one, man," he whispered.

James looked at him sternly. "Nick, you have the potential to be a great leader. You must be given a chance to lead." His face softened as he smiled. "I trust you."

"Thanks, man," Nick said, standing up a little taller.

"Now that that's settled. I think it's about time that you go home and rest up," said Dr. Gabrielle. "We'll discuss strategy tomorrow afternoon. You are dismissed. Good job today."

***

At school the next day, a few more students and faculty members seemed ill. They were pale with sunken eyes, and they looked completely exhausted. A student passing by coughed in front of James, and he about had a conniption.

"Abby, has your issue plagued the entire school?" he asked, breathing into his shirt.

She looked around. "I don't think so. These guys look a whole lot worse than I do. I just have the sneezing and runny nose, but some of these people look like they have a case of death warmed over."

"That is not an actual disease," James commented.

"I guess you're not too freaked out to correct me," she said, rolling her eyes.

"I will never be that *freaked out*," he said. His voice was muffled by his shirt.

Abby crossed her arms. "I'm actually feeling better today."

As I looked around, I noticed something. "Hey, guys?"

"Wha iph ih, Kerry?" asked Nick as he was downing a pop tart.

I pointed at Cody Sharpe, a kid on the lacrosse team. He looked like he hadn't gotten any sleep in days. He was carrying around four bottles of Wacky Water. I looked at another kid, a freshman, who had three bottles. He looked just as bad. "Everyone that's sick, they're all carrying Wacky Water."

"Everyone is carrying around Wacky Water, except for us," James said.

"I mean they're carrying around a lot of bottles," I said.

James looked around. He was hard to take seriously, though, because he was still holding his shirt up to his nose. "I noticed that yesterday with Mr. Simmons and Greg. They were drinking an excessive amount of Wacky

Water, and they seemed a little unwell. It is possible the two things are connected…potential evidence that we may indeed be dealing with a Corrupted. That, or Wacky Water is contaminated somehow. We need to get a sample of it and take some tests at the lab."

Abby watched a girl with a bottle of Wacky Water in each hand walk by and wrinkled her nose. "Shouldn't be too hard, the stuff is everywhere."

We walked into homeroom. There were a few students hacking and coughing in their seats, as pale as the grave. Every class had students that were sick, but nobody was absent. And the way that they were acting, it was like they didn't realize they were sick.

At lunch, the line at the vending machines was backed up clear to the stairs. And they were all getting Wacky Water. Those that looked the sickest bought the most bottles. Nick managed to grab the last one. He ran back to the lunch table and handed the bottle to James.

James grabbed a large plastic bag with the word *EVIDENCE* spread across it from his backpack. "Alright," he said as he held the bag open. "Place the evidence in the bag. I should have given you gloves. We do not want the evidence any more compromised than it already is."

"Where did you get the bag from?" asked Abby. "Did you steal it from a police station?"

James shook his head. "From the Edania Organization. They had some extra, so I asked if I could take a few. You never know when they might come in handy."

I hit his bookbag. "With all of your evidence bags and disinfectant spray, do you have any room for your actual school stuff?"

He looked insulted. "Of course I do. What kind of person do you think I am?"

"You're right," I said. "*Totally* crazy question."

James examined the bottle inside of the evidence bag, turning it around and squinting at it. It had an image of Wacky William holding a giant strawberry. "We need to take this to the organization immediately after school. I will run as many tests as I can, and hopefully we will find an answer."

***

The rest of the day, you would have thought we were in some kind of zombie apocalypse, because some of the students and even a few teachers were walking around like the living dead. Luckily, they were craving more Wacky Water and not brains. Everyone seemed to be on edge since the school had run out of the stuff.

After school, we headed straight for the Edania Organization and went to the lab. James used his I.D. card to sign in. He skipped joyfully over to an exam table and donned a pair of gloves. He grabbed a beaker and a centrifuge tube and uncapped the bottle of Wacky Water. He measured it out and poured some water into both containers, put the tube in the centrifuge and spun it at its highest speed.

"That should take ten minutes to spin," James said, completely immersed in what he was doing. "In the meantime…" He grabbed a pipette and placed a drop of Wacky Water onto a slide, put a coverslip on it, and started to look at it under the microscope. "Kelly," he said.

"What?" I answered.

He handed me the bottle of Wacky Water. "Would you please prepare a slide and put some Gram stain on it?"

"Um. What?" I said.

He pointed at the cabinet closest to the door. "There is a bottle on the second shelf there that says *Gram stain*. If you could please put a drop of Wacky Water on the slide, then put a drop of the stain on top of it and put the cover slip on."

I rolled my eyes. This brought me back to when we were in elementary school and he made me play mad scientist's assistant. "Fine," I answered.

"Oh, and could you also run a sample of the water through the mass spectrometer down the hall?"

Nick's eyes got wide. "The massive whatometer?"

James glanced up at him from the microscope. "It's a machine that determines the elemental signature of a sample and reveals the chemical identity or structure of the chemical compounds found within it."

"And you want Kelly to run it?" Abby said, looking at me sympathetically. "Why don't you do it? You're the brainiac."

"I'm currently looking at this sample," he said. "And I'll be looking at the Gram stain next. I just want us to work as efficiently as possible."

I put my hands up. "It's okay, I got it. I guess I'll be right back."

"What should me and Abbs do?" Nick asked as I left the room.

"Go find Dr. Gabrielle and ask for her to come here," I heard James say, sounding a little impatient.

I walked down the hall with the bottle of Wacky Water and stopped at the door that said *Chemical Analysis Lab*. I swiped my card and walked in.

There were several machines and microscopes in here. Looking around, I wondered how many times James had been in here, and how many of the machines he'd used. On the lab table closest to me, there was a square machine about the size of a banker's box. A blue label was slapped onto its front: *EDANIA-CORP. MASS-SPECTRO1000*. I guessed that was the mass spectrometer thingy. Luckily, it came with detailed instructions. I followed each step as best as I could, scared that I might break it or blow the lab up or something. Finally, I hit the little green button, and the screen said *Analyzing*. With a sigh of relief, I left the room and joined the others back in the biology lab.

"You took too long," James said, looking into the microscope. "I'm looking at the Gram stain slide now."

"Fine," I said sarcastically. "Just have the party without me."

He smiled while examining the slide. "I *did* leave some of the sample for you to run a tox-screen."

"You did?" I said with even more sarcasm. "You shouldn't have."

"The toxicology analysis machine is in the same room as the mass spectrometer," James said as he flicked his hand in a *shoo* gesture. "We must hurry if we want to find answers before more people get sick."

My eyebrows just about hit the ceiling. I had half a mind to chuck the bottle at his big head, but I thought better of it. He was always like this when he was in his element. So, I sighed and went back to the chemical analysis lab.

I found the tox-screen machine and carefully read the instructions about how to use it and placed the specimen in the machine. After a moment, it started to hum.

"So, is there anything of interest?" asked Dr. Gabrielle as she walked into the room.

I shrugged. "I just started it up. But I hope we find *something* to explain why everyone is getting sick." I tried to hide my worry, but I couldn't. "You should have seen the kids at school, they looked awful. The more Wacky Water they drink, the sicker they seem to get."

She looked at me solemnly. "Well, I hope we get our answer. Let's go see if James has found anything."

I followed her back to the biology lab. Nick was spinning around on one of the wheeled chairs and Abby was filing her nails.

"Hey, guys!" said Nick, still spinning. "I think J-Man is broken. He keeps whispering to himself."

James was typing something into a computer tablet and muttering, which was what he did when he couldn't come to a conclusion about something. "Let's see, if there were no Gram-positive or negative bacteria of concern…and I could not find anything on the electron microscope, so there are no viruses. I also did not see any protozoa, fungi or any other contaminating agents. Perhaps it's some kind of toxin or chemical? I suppose we will have to wait until the mass spectrometer and the tox-screen are finished with their analyses to determine that. I saw absolutely nothing of suspicion…except for the fact that—"

"So, James. What's the news?" asked Dr. Gabrielle, who looked annoyed that he did not even look up when we walked in.

He glanced over at the doctor. "Hmm? Oh, right. So, I could not find anything microscopically that would indicate any infectious agents. Although I did notice something strange."

She tapped her foot impatiently. "And that would be?"

"The way the water looked microscopically," he said. He held up the beaker that had some of the water still in it. "To the naked eye, it looks like ordinary water. However, when you look at it under magnification, you will see that it has a strange consistency. It is slightly thicker than normal water. I checked its specific gravity, and it was higher than your typical flavored bottled water."

"What is the consequence of the water's specific gravity?" asked Dr. Gabrielle.

He thought for a moment. "It could indicate that there are some ingredients in there that would make the water heavier, like lead or something. It depends on what the other tests show. Another oddity is how the water moved under the slide. It seemed to move around in some kind of pattern, almost like I was looking at some kind of giant, unicellular organism."

"Like the water is a living thing?" I asked.

James nodded. "Indeed, but such things are improbable."

Dr. Gabrielle tapped her chin. "With Dark-Segols, you never know. You should know that by now, what with the mutant bugs, the illusion-casting tree, the plant woman—"

James removed the slide from the microscope and threw it away in the sharps container. "I understand. Things that are not rational in the natural world may not apply when it comes to Segols… We'll get more answers when we get the tox screen and the mass spec results." He typed something on the tablet, and the test results from both machines popped up on the tv screen in the lab.

Nick squinted at the screen. "It all looks like Greek to me. What's all that sciencey scribble mean?"

James reviewed the results carefully. "Hmm, no toxins, no chemicals, no contagions detected," he said. "Rather boring test results. This is quite the mystery."

"I'll run all of this information by Steph and see what she thinks," said Dr. Gabrielle. "You are dismissed. We will come up with some sort of plan tomorrow, so we should have a reliable tactical plan by next week."

"Next week?" Abby repeated, her eyes wide.

Dr. Gabrielle looked over at her. "Yes, good plans take time. I want to make sure that the four of you come up with a good one instead of just jumping in without any idea of what you're getting yourself into."

Abby threw her hands down. "But what about all of the kids at school who are getting sick from drinking that stuff?" she said. *Did she get possessed by Nick?* "And who knows how many others across the islands? What if some of them die while we're here twiddling our thumbs?"

Dr. Gabrielle seemed unmoved on the issue. "I understand your point, but we must exercise caution. Whoever or whatever we're dealing with has exceptional power, and you can't afford to jump into the fray half-cocked."

Abby sighed. "Whatever, fine," she said as she walked out of the lab.

"Sorry, Doc," said Nick with an apologetic shrug. "She really wants to get this over with so she can get the Ark and be able to control her superpower better." *Did Nick and Abby just switch bodies or something?* "But I can tell she's also worried about everyone who's drinking that stuff."

"Believe me, I get it…" Dr. Gabrielle said. "It's frustrating when faced with trials such as these, but we must use our heads if we're to best this evil. Do you understand, Nicklaus?"

He nodded. "I do, but at the same time, I wish we could do something about it now. This water is hurting people, and it's not like they'll believe us if we tell 'em it's bad for them. Everyone seems to be addicted to the stuff."

Dr. Gabrielle smiled. "I have no doubt that you will come up with something. You do have quite the team. James is bright and intelligent, Kelly seems to have the level head, and Abby is determined." She crossed her arms and looked deep into Nick's eyes. "And, although you can be aggravating, I think you have a potential to be one of the greatest leaders this organization has seen in a while."

He blushed. "Me? Nah, I don't think so."

She seemed to be filled with understanding all of a sudden. "You just need the experience, and I think this specific mission will be the perfect opportunity for you to gain it. Just remember to think before you leap."

He saluted her. "You got it, Dr. Shortstuff."

She sighed in annoyance. "Go, get out of here. I'll see you tomorrow."

***

The next day, we had a few absences from school. Mrs. Juris, the school nurse, said that everyone who was sent home seemed to have been drained of all of their energy, which is something she said she had never seen before. But the truth was that she had seen something similar with the mantis infestation, but for some reason, she and everyone else had forgotten about the incident, at least the part about the bugs being mutants that sucked the energy out of you…lucky them.

Something that wasn't seen with the mantis attack, though, was that those who were absent now also had low temperatures and coughing fits. Greg from history class was in the emergency room for his illness. His girlfriend told us that his brain was swollen, and he kept coming in and out of consciousness. The doctors told his family that there was a chance that he could die. Nobody had connected Wacky Water to the illnesses; they thought that there was just some nasty influenza or meningitis outbreak.

At lunch, Abby was vehement about taking immediate action.

"Nick, we have to do something! Greg could die because of this, and who knows how many other people are going to get hurt?"

"We will, sis," Nick said, poking his taco salad with a fork. "But the doc said that we need to be careful with this one."

She sighed. "Since when are you careful about anything?"

"I'm tryin' here," he said, sounding miserable. "I don't want any of you to get hurt because I made a stupid decision."

She slammed her hands on the table. "This isn't just the school or a remote part of the woods in danger this time. All of the Force-Pointe Islands are in trouble, and what if Wacky Water is distributed worldwide?"

James raised his hand. "I would have to agree with her. Seeing the devastation this Wacky Water is causing issues immediate action. However, I suggest doing some more investigation before confronting this unknown foe."

"So, you think we should go to the water factory again tonight and do some sleuthing?" Abby said. "I bet nobody will be there after dark, anyway." *She really must be anxious to get this Ark. She was never this energetic about our missions.*

James nodded. "I suppose it does limit the risks of getting caught."

Nick thought for a moment. "Let's at least call Dr. Shortstuff to let her know."

Abby rolled her eyes. "Do we need to let her know every time we do something?"

Nick shook his head. "No, but we should let her know just in case."

Abby patted James's back. "C'mon, bro. Even James is okay with the plan, and he's Mr. Careful."

Nick looked at me. "What do *you* think, Kelly?"

*Oh no…I don't want to be put in the middle of this! But…his handsome green eyes…* "I think we should call Dr. Gabrielle at least," I suggested.

"Alright then," he said with a smile. "That's what we'll do."

Abby slapped her hand on the table again. "Come on, guys. How about we just message Dr. Gabrielle, and if she messages back saying not to go, then we won't. This could be an opportunity to get the Ark from under the bad guys' noses."

Nick was deep in thought for a moment, which was a flattering look for him with the clenched jaw and thoughtful eyes. He looked at Abby. "Fine, we'll go take a quick look."

Abby let out a relieved sigh.

Nick turned to me, his face tense. "You okay with this?"

I nodded. "I guess we shouldn't have too much trouble if we just take a quick look. And as long as we message Dr. Gabrielle." Although, I really didn't like the idea, thinking back to Hotel Barbaas. I really felt like we should think it through more, but Abby and James seemed to be on a mission, and I didn't want to stress Nick out by being the voice of contention.

***

We waited for the sun to set before we headed to Wacky Water World to break into the factory. We missed our appointed time to go check in with Dr. Gabrielle, but she didn't message anyone to scold us for it. As we drove along Soraya Woods, Abby sent Dr. Gabrielle a message to let her know where we were going, but she didn't answer back. Nick parked just outside of the Wacky Water World's parking lot.

"Alright, what is the plan exactly?" I asked as we got out of the car.

"We break into the factory," James said calmly, like we weren't totally about to break the law. "To do that, we will require Kelly's electrical Segol to disable the security system."

Nick had a goofy smile on his face. "You mean she's gotta use her Angel's Bolt?" James nodded and opened his mouth to continue.

"Wait, wait, wait," I interrupted. "I can only get it to work like, ten percent of the time even in training. And I have very little control over it when it does work."

"You're good, Kelly. We're here to back you up," said Nick with that same goofy smile.

*Ugh…why does he have to do that? It's so hard to say no to him when he smiles at me like that.* I sighed. "I'll give it a try, but if I cause an explosion, it's not my fault."

James nodded. "Duly noted. Now let's get a move on. I do not wish to be here longer than we have to be."

"Absolutely!" said Abby with urgency in her voice. "Let's just get what we came here for and get out."

Nick ran his finger down Abby's neck. "What's wrong, Abbs? Think that clown guy is gonna pop up out of nowhere and get ya?" he whispered creepily.

She slapped the back of her neck and cringed. Then she turned around and punched Nick on the shoulder. "Stop it, Nick!"

He shrugged. "Hey, it was your idea to come here."

She looked like she was about to kick him. "I know, but that's just because we need to get the Ark and see what's up with this Wacky Water."

We approached the park's entrance. The air was still, and the night was silent, which made the waterpark even creepier under the black and silent cloak of night.

"Aren't you worried about security cameras?" Nick asked.

James shook his head. "My Scan ability did not pick up any cameras throughout the entire area, but their security system is pretty efficient."

"You can do all that?" Nick asked, impressed. "Looks like your superpower is growing."

James blushed. "I had some help from the Edania Organization's computer. Gideon showed me how to use my Scan ability alongside the organization's computer to sort of download things into my mind…but I did get a particularly painful headache from it. I think I overdid it a little bit."

We snuck to the side of the building, where there was a large electrical box that had FORCE-POINTE SECURITY inscribed across it.

James crept up to the box and examined it. "Luckily, it's only the inside of the building that has it installed." He looked at me. "Alright, Kelly, are you ready?"

"Do I have to?" I asked as I took a step back.

"You are the only one who can," he said. "My Segol can only link up to the Edania Organization's computer, Abby's temporal immobilization ability would only help for a minute or two, and Nick's fire power will no doubt cause attention. If you do this just right, it will short-circuit the security system and allow us to enter the building without being detected."

I slowly walked toward the electrical box. "Okay, okay…I'll try."

"It needs to be strong enough so that it quickly short-circuits the system, but weak enough so that it doesn't completely fry it," James said, like it was no big deal. *I'd like to see him try it…*

I gathered my confidence, put my hand on the security system's electrical box, and closed my eyes. *Alright, Kelly, you can do this, you just have to concentrate.* My hands felt warm, which was a good sign.

"Good job, Ms. Kelly, it's working!" yelled Nick.

My hands felt warmer and warmer as the electricity surged through them, I opened my eyes and both of them were surrounded by a golden electrical current. But I needed to lower the power a little; the circuit was making a loud buzzing sound like it was going to fry at any second. I took a deep breath and the electrical current lessened.

There was a quiet *zap* sound that came from the inside of the power box.

"I think that did the trick," I said.

"One way to find out," said James.

We walked around to the entrance to the indoor part of the park.

I took out a bobby pin and jimmied the lock. "Alright, Nick, do you think you can slide the door open?" I asked.

Nick cracked his knuckles. "Stand aside, ma'am. This requires some muscle!"

He pulled the sliding doors open as James, Abby, and I walked through the entrance, and Nick followed after.

"This place is even creepier at night," said Abby as her eyes darted around anxiously. "Let's just get this done so I can have the Ark to control my power better…and find out what's going on with the Wacky Water stuff, of course…"

"You sure are selfless, sis," Nick commented.

"Hey, I'm trying to be…" she said indignantly. "I mean, what good am I as an agent if I can't even control my power?"

Nick swatted at her. "Yeah, yeah. Let's get this done."

James pointed toward the Tunnel of Love stairwell. "We need to head up there. That's where the entrance to the factory is."

The sign above the stairwell glowed an eerie red color, which made the white tiles on the stairs look crimson as well.

We made our way up the stairs. It was dead silent, which didn't make me feel any better. I walked up to the door at the end of the room and got to my knees to pick the lock. The lock clicked. But I didn't get a chance to open the door.

I gasped as water leaked through the bottom of the door. Before I could get up, a powerful aqua jet shot up from the puddle and knocked me away from the door.

Nick helped me up. "You okay?"

Before I could answer, the jet of water stopped, and a woman was standing in the puddle of water. It was Marina. She was even prettier in person. Her long hair was jet black and silky, and her sapphire eyes shimmered like twin pools of crystal. Her skin was pale and flawless. She wore a blue kimono with wave patterns sewn into it.

"My, my, my, what do we have here…trespassers?" she said in an eerily calm voice.

The four of us backed away toward the stairs. Marina sighed as her body melted into the puddle of water. A moment later, another jet of water shot up from right behind us. Marina appeared as the water subsided. "First you break into my lovely park uninvited, and now you are trying to leave without even trying to hold a conversation? How positively uncivilized. Just what are they teaching you at that dreadful organization?"

"Abby," I whispered. "Try to freeze her."

Abby nodded and lifted her hands.

"Tsk, tsk. There will be none of that!" said Marina as she threw a glowing ball of water at Abby.

When the water hit her, it expanded, and Abby was suddenly trapped behind a wall of water. She tried desperately to get out, but something kept her from escaping, like she was behind an invisible wall.

Marina hmphed. "How rude to raise your hand against a proper lady. You need to be locked up…yes! Locked up like a trapped fish."

Abby tried to claw her way through the invisible wall, but she couldn't get out! I ran to her and tried to pull her out, but the wall of water felt as solid as steel.

"Let her go!" Nick yelled, infuriated.

Marina glared at him, her bright eyes darkening into gray pools. "It's not gentlemanly of you to shout demands."

Nick stepped toward her. "I said, let her go!"

She covered her ears and winced. "Yes, yes. I heard you the first time. But I think I will let the little wretch drown in my pool of sorrow. And as for the three of you…" She snapped her fingers, and three more jets of water shot up from the ground. Suddenly, we were staring three huge, heavily-muscled men in the face.

Marina giggled. "Take care of this rabble, boys. I am sick of them poisoning the very air with their boorish presence."

One of them grabbed James, and another grabbed me. The last tried to grab Nick, but he knocked him hard to the ground. When the man landed, he liquified into a giant puddle of water.

"Oh, how rude!" said Marina indignantly.

Nick glared at her, fire burning in his eyes. Marina suddenly looked like she was in pain. Her whole body started to steam and boil. Suddenly, she exploded, and water sprayed all over the place.

The men holding me and James melted into puddles, and Abby's watery prison splashed loudly onto the floor. Abby fell to her knees. We ran to her.

"Are you okay, Abbs?" Nick asked as he helped her up.

She hacked and gasped. "Y-yeah. Looks like you really took care of that evil little mermaid."

"He most certainly did not!" Marina's voice echoed.

We looked back toward the stairwell, and Marina shot up out of the puddle she'd made when she blew up. "It will take more than brute force to defeat me. I may be a delicate little water flower, but this flower has thorns. I'm more than a match for you peasants!"

Nick stepped toward her and made a large fireball.

"I believe it's time to douse those flames of yours, handsome," she said with cold calm. She waved her hand, and a pillar of water lifted Nick up six feet in the air. His whole body was submerged except for his head and he struggled to move. "Let go of me, you sea hag!" he yelled.

Marina's eyes became cold and demented. "I believe it's time to teach you a lesson, sir. You cannot go around throwing insults at your superiors." She glanced over toward the slide. "I believe I must make an example of you."

She strutted over to the slide and held her hand over it, and water started gushing out of the jets as the slide came to life. She knelt over it and touched it with her finger, and the water started to bubble. The pressure intensified and started to glow.

She got up and pointed her hand at the pillar of water Nick was trapped in, and it started to move across the room.

Abby, James, and I tried to run to him, but a giant wall of water shot up in front of us. It was as crystal clear as ice and as hard as stone.

Marina looked up at Nick, and a thin, wicked smile crept onto her face. "Time to take a ride down the Tunnel of Love, I do hope you enjoy it." She threw her hand toward the slide, and the pillar crashed like a tidal wave into the bubbling water.

Nick yelled as he flew down into the darkness.

"Nick!" I yelled. I could hear him screaming in pain as his voice slowly started to fade. Tears started to sting my eyes.

Marina walked through the wall of crystalline water and grinned at us. She held her hand out, and a bright ball of light appeared right above it. She looked at me and giggled. "Your boyfriend is caught in my torrent of energy-sapping water. What is floating before you is his energy." The ball of light quickly became larger and brighter. "And as you can see, his energy is draining fast. Yes, and as he fights with all his might to stay above water, it will only drain him faster."

"How…how could you do such a thing?" Abby yelled, her voice hoarse with hatred.

Marina frowned. "He's the one who attacked me first, after breaking into my property." She held out her other hand right below the ball of light. "Oh, dearie me. He certainly has a lot of energy. I've never seen so much come from one person."

The ball of energy was getting so bright that it was blinding.

Marina giggled again. "I suppose I should thank you for breaking into my lovely park. I've gotten more energy out of that adorable, brutish boy than I've gotten out of everyone else combined. I'll have the Ark's barrier shattered by morning.

"To show my appreciation, I will let you collect the body of your fallen comrade. He should be a lifeless shell by now, gracefully floating in the water below. And may this be a lesson, dears. Do not think to interfere with me again, or you'll be joining him in death." With those final words, Marina and the brilliant ball of light vanished behind a veil of water.

The three of us scrambled down the stairs toward the giant pool in the building's lower level. We reached the pool and searched for Nick. We saw him floating off in the distance, his arm was wrapped around the safety rope that divided the exit of the slide with the rest of the pool.

We frantically ran toward him, stumbling in the water as we tried to make it to him. Horrible thoughts were running through my mind. *What if he's…no. He can't be!* When we reached him, I turned him over. He wasn't moving, and his skin was pale.

# CHAPTER 6: DROWNING—ABBY

We frantically tried pulling Nick out of the water, but I could hardly muster up the strength. *How could this have happened?* I thought as we pulled Nick closer toward the pool's edge.

At long last, we got him out of the pool. We laid him down on the ground. His lips were pale, and it didn't look like he was breathing. He wasn't moving at all.

I could hardly stand, I was so frantic. Looking at my brother like that…so helpless, it made me sick to my stomach.

James checked the pulse of his wrist. He looked up at me and Kelly with a tired and defeated smile. "He has a pulse, but it's very weak." He put his ear to Nick's mouth. "But I can't… I don't think he's breathing."

"Can't you do CPR or something?" I yelled.

"I—I can't," he said, his voice shaking. "I haven't been properly—"

Kelly got on the floor and sat right above Nick. "Move, James," she said quickly. She tilted Nick's head back and opened his mouth. She gave two breaths, then she put her ear to his mouth. "Still not breathing…" She gave him two more breaths.

"Please, God. Let him be okay…" I prayed.

She listened again, then gave him two more breaths.

James sat next to Nick, rocking back and forth.

Kelly listened again, and gave two more breaths. Nick's chest twitched, and he hacked up a lot of water. He was struggling to breathe, and he was still unconscious.

After he was done hacking, Kelly listened to his chest again. "He's breathing, but barely. We need to get him to a hospital."

"An ambulance would not make it here in time. Too many back roads," James said, still rocking.

"We're going to have to drive him," I said.

The three of us carefully picked him up and tried to move as quickly as we could without dropping him. We made our way down the hallway with the creepy animatronics behind the windows. I glanced over at the one of Wacky William, and I could have sworn it winked at me. A small squeak left my mouth as I looked forward. I couldn't get freaked. Not now. Just then, something even worse ran through my mind. What would we do if we ran into Marina again? What if she found out Nick was still alive? Would she come back to finish the job? I shook those thoughts away. I had to focus on getting Nick out of here.

Finally, we made it outside. It was getting harder and harder to carry him, but we had to. We *had* to.

We placed him gently on the pavement and I got the keys from his pocket and unlocked the door. Kelly jumped in the back seat, and we laid him across the seat, putting his head on her lap. James got in the front seat and I hopped into the driver's side. I started the car and drove out of there as fast as I could.

"Should we take him to the Edania Organization?" I asked shakily, trying to keep it together.

"It's too far," Kelly said, her voice trembling. "Go to Force-Pointe General Hospital. It's right on the other side of the bridge." I looked at her through the rearview mirror. She was holding Nick gently, stroking his hair, crying.

"Alright," I said. "Tell me where to go."

"Turn left at the light," James said.

"You sure?" I said, glancing over at him. "You're terrible at directions." I thought about the time James directed Nick to a closet instead of the bathroom in his own house.

"I've found that my Segol is a good remedy for that," he answered.

I turned left just as the light turned red and got honked at by a few cars. *Let them honk.*

"Keep left and get on route thirty," James said. "It will take us straight to the hospital." He spoke in his normal, calculating voice, but his face was haunted with worry.

I floored it all the way to the hospital and parked in the ER parking lot as close as I could to the hospital's entrance, which was about halfway to the hospital. The parking lot was pretty full; the ER must've be packed… That sent a wave of anxiety over me. What if they couldn't see Nick? What if they couldn't help him? I tried to cast the thoughts aside; this was no time for an anxiety attack.

James and I got out of the car and we pushed our seats forward. We picked Nick up from the back seat. He was still unresponsive.

"He's still breathing," said Kelly, her hazel eyes red and puffy from crying.

"Wait a moment," said James, looking down at Nick suspiciously. "He is dry as a bone. He should be soaking wet."

Kelly got out of the car. "It's weird, on the way over here the water seemed to seep into his skin."

That's when I noticed that we were *all* dry. But we couldn't dwell on that now. We had to get Nick inside.

We started making our way toward the ER as quickly as possible, but we were really struggling the closer we got. He didn't look it, but he was pretty heavy. But it seemed a little more than that. I felt totally exhausted all of a sudden, like my cold was getting worse. My body started to ache and I felt lightheaded.

We finally made it into the hospital.

"Somebody, help!" I yelled.

The three of us couldn't take the weight anymore, and we dropped to the floor.

A young female nurse ran toward us, looking horrified. "What happened?"

We couldn't answer, we were all so out of breath. An older nurse rushed over. She assessed Nick's condition. "It looks like another case. This one's bad," she said worriedly.

The younger nurse nodded and looked at us. "I'm going to call for a doctor. I will be right back." She ran to the reception desk and picked up the phone. She was trying to talk quietly. "Yes, doctor…it looks like another case has just come in…no, he's not ambulatory, he's not even conscious…yes, he was carried in by three young people…it looks pretty bad…alright…alright…I don't know if that'll be any help, he's practically a D.O.A.…yes…no…thank you, Doctor…I'll let them know." She hung up and walked toward us. "They're heading down now. Don't worry, we'll do our best to save him."

The large double-doors on the far side of the waiting room swung open, and four men ran through the doors pushing a gurney. They walked toward us, and the men knelt down, picked Nick up and laid him on the gurney. They started to wheel him away, and the three of us followed. We made it to the door when the nurse who made the call stopped us. "I'm sorry, you can't come in here. Only family is allowed past this point."

"I'm his sister!" I snapped.

She blinked at me. "Alright, you can come. But the other two have to stay here."

"That's *so* not happening," I said with so much anger that I was starting to scare myself. "They're coming too!"

"It's okay, Abby. Go, we will see him later," James whispered.

Kelly put her hand on my shoulder. "He needs someone with him right now. Go…" I could see fresh tears start to form in her worried and tired eyes.

I took a deep breath and nodded. "Okay, but I'll get you guys as soon as I can."

I followed the nurse into the long hallway. I could hear the large automated doors slam behind me, which made me jump a little. The nurse rushed me into a room. A male doctor was listening to Nick with his stethoscope as the technicians connected a bunch of wires to him.

"Severe bradycardia, twenty…five BPM." He listened to his lungs. "Very weak and shallow breaths." He looked at the monitor that just turned on. "Temperature is ninety-eight point nine, blood pressure is eighty-five over fifty." He opened Nick's eyelid and shined a light in his pupil. "Eyes unresponsive…" He lightly slapped his cheek. "Excuse me, young man, can you hear me? You're in the hospital, we're going to do our best to help you…" He paused. "This is not good, his skin is slightly cyanotic."

I looked at Nick; his skin did look a little blue. I started to tear up. I winced as I tried to keep the tears back. The doctor looked over at me and headed my way.

"Are you a relative of his?" he asked.

I looked at him, barely able to stand, but I did manage to nod. "I'm—I'm his twin sister."

He smiled at me warmly, which made me even more upset. *How can he be so calm when my brother is over there like that?* "I'm Dr. Bennett," he said, then he frowned. "To tell you the truth, your brother is not doing very well. It looks like his body is starting to shut down. We'll do our best, but at first glance, he does have a very guarded prognosis."

"What are you saying?" I asked, looking at the doctor like he was speaking a different language.

He couldn't look me in the eye. "To be honest, your brother may die. He's showing similar symptoms of several other youths and a few adults that have some mysterious illness. One of them has died already, and your brother looks worse than they did."

"B-but my brother *can't* die!" I yelled.

"I realize that this is upsetting," he said, and I couldn't tell if he was being genuine or if it was just part of the script he had to say when stuff like this happened. "But it's an unfortunate possibility. We'll try to stabilize him. But, honestly, even if we can, it'll be a long road for him."

"This is all my fault," I whispered. I was appalled at myself.

"We all feel that way, miss," Dr. Bennett said solemnly as he put his hand on my shoulder. "I know how you feel."

I jerked away from him. "How could you possibly know how I feel?"

He took a step back. He still had the same disgusting look of sympathy on his face. "Whenever something tragic happens to a loved one, oftentimes we blame ourselves. But this was an unforeseen circumstance. I don't know what's causing this illness. I don't know if it's something they accidently ingested, if it's some kind of infectious disease, or if it's drug related—"

"*Drug* related?" I screamed. "Do you really think my brother would do something so stupid? He's not on drugs!"

He held his hands up in surrender. "Calm down, miss. I wasn't trying to imply that he is, but I need to narrow the cause down. If it's something they accidently ingested, I need to find out what. If it's infectious, then that's an entirely different story… I would have to initiate a quarantine of this hospital and call in the specialists."

I rolled my eyes. *Clearly, nobody knows what's going on here. They haven't connected*

*Wacky Water to this illness. And it's not like I could tell the doctor what was really happening to them, because then he would think I was insane.* I took a deep breath so I wouldn't kill the doctor. "Listen, my brother is a good person…the best I've ever known. Sure, his obnoxious optimism and cheeriness get on my nerves sometimes. But…the world would be a terrible place without him in it. So please, do everything you can to save him."

"You have my promise," the doctor said.

"I have two friends that want to see him," I said. "They're out in the waiting room. How long until they can come in?"

"It's hard to say," he answered. "I want to make sure he's stabilized first. So, why don't you go back to the waiting room and join them? I'll be sure to let you know as soon as you all can visit him."

I looked at Nick lying there on the hospital bed. I had never seen him look so helpless. I didn't see my brave, strong, confident brother on the table; I saw a poor, frail, weak boy fighting for his life. I looked back at the doctor and nodded.

I made my way back to the waiting room. My ears were ringing. The room was spinning. I couldn't take it anymore. When I saw Kelly and James walk toward me, I started to sob. Kelly embraced me.

"It's going to be okay, Abby. He'll pull through this, you'll see," she said, but her voice cracked.

"I don't know if he will. The doctor said that it's possible that he could—" My crying worsened. "This is all my fault!"

"Don't say that," Kelly whispered.

"You know it's true," I said as I gently pushed her off of me. "I'm the one that just *had* to get the Ark as soon as possible without a plan. Nick didn't really want to go. He wanted to talk to Dr. Gabrielle about it. But no, I said, 'Why don't we just message her?'. He could die because of me!"

"I believe I am to blame," said James. He was staring at the floor and looked like he felt just as guilty as I did.

"How could it be your fault?" I asked.

His whole body was trembling. "You may have suggested going, but I was the one that told him that everything would be fine…that I had a plan. Although, I had no plan…and that monstrous woman… If I had a plan, he may not be in the condition he's in now. He—he trusted me, and I failed. I failed as the tactician, and worse…I failed as a friend…" He turned away from us and took off his glasses.

Kelly and I hugged him.

"It's going to be alright," I said, hoping I wasn't lying. "Nick's a fighter. He won't let something like this keep him down."

"I pray you are correct," James said in a hushed tone. "I called Dr. Stephani, hoping Nick could be transferred to the Edania Organization's hospital. Naturally, they would be much better equipped to treat a Dark-Segol related illness. But she said that the Force-Pointe Island government is instituting a state of emergency within the hour. Nobody in this hospital will be able to leave, which means they can't even be transferred to another facility."

"What's that mean?" I asked.

He sighed. "They think it may be some kind of infectious disease. They're going to try to contain it by blocking off this hospital. Anyone who is showing similar symptoms to people like Greg, or Mr. Simmons, or Nick…they are supposed to come here so they do not contaminate any other hospital. But this isn't an infectious disease, not exactly. It has to do with that vile water, and nobody seems to have picked up on it."

Sirens started blaring outside, then several gurneys were rushed in, carrying patients. I recognized some of them from school. Most of them were awake, but a few were not. They were all rushed through the doors into the ER.

James squinted his eyes as he looked out of the window. "It looks like they are serious about the quarantine." He pointed outside, where several men in hazmat suits were putting up some sort of blockade around the hospital. "They are about to completely block us in until they can verify that whatever is going on is not infectious, or it has been contained and eliminated, should it be a disease." He started to tremble again. "So, in other words, we are stuck in this hospital until then…stuck in this breeding ground for nosocomial infections."

"But we need to get out so we can go to the organization and tell them about what's going on," said Kelly.

"Excuse me," said Dr. Bennet, who was walking toward us from the double doors.

The three of us faced him.

He had that same pleasant look on his face, but my urge to slap it off of him was almost gone. "I realize what's going on around here is a bit scary. But it's for the best. At any rate, we were able to at least stabilize your brother. His heart rate and blood pressure are much lower than I would like, but he is breathing on his own. If you three follow me, you can see him."

We followed him back to Nick's hospital room. On our way, I saw that most rooms had at least two people in them. Luckily, Nick was in a small, single-patient room.

As we walked in, James asked the doctor a question.

"Why aren't you wearing a hazmat suit or other P.P.E. if we are under a quarantine for a potential infectious disease?"

The Dr. picked up a chart and started reading through it. "I've already been in contact with several of these patients. If they have something I am sure to get it. Anyway, it looks like we're all going to be stuck here for a little while. So, I'll let you kids stay in here with your friend."

James was frowning. "It's not that we're ungrateful, but what about protocol? Are you not going to separate the obviously ailing individuals from the apparently healthy?"

Dr. Bennett shook his head. "Truthfully, I don't believe it's infectious. And your friend needs all the support he can get right now." I started to believe in that warm smile of his. "Now, if you'll excuse me, I need to check on the other patients." He left Nick's room and shut the door.

James grunted. "Where did that doctor get his license, a cereal box? You cannot be so sentimental in an emergency like this. What if this *was* an outbreak of a virulent disease? He would have the whole hospital infected with that attitude!"

"James, get over it!" Kelly said with a little too much sass. "It's not an infectious disease, so get your crazy under control!"

"I apologize," he whispered.

Kelly looked at Nick. She put her hand over her mouth. "Oh, Nick…"

James was looking around the room for something.

"What are you doing?" I asked.

"Well, this doctor is obviously a slight bit irresponsible…" he said. "Perhaps he left bloodwork results or something in the room. I would like to personally review them. I may not be much help in most circumstances, but when it comes to things like this, I know I can do my part."

He found a clipboard with some papers on it. "Aha, here we go." He skimmed through the report. "Hmm. 'Patient arrived unconscious. Has slight cyanosis, low BP…similar symptoms as at least seven other patients. Although patient is the worst so far, he is not hypothermic like all the others, his temperature is normal… As for cause, I suspect accidental ingestion of unknown toxin. Potential differentials may be infectious disease, but unlikely…more probable differential is drug overdose…' Wait, drug overdose? Ridiculous!"

I stomped my foot. "That's what I said!"

"Still," he said, looking at the chart. "The doctor doesn't know him. And drug abuse is an unfortunate epidemic even in the Force-Pointe Islands."

"What does the bloodwork show?" Kelly asked.

James flipped through the medical report. "Let's see, bloodwork…bloodwork. Ah, here it is. Oh," he said, his eyebrows furrowed.

"Oh. What?" I asked, hoping not to get the answer I was thinking.

He stared at the paper. "It isn't good. His iron, hemoglobin, and glucose levels are dangerously low. His RBC count is just under normal, and his WBC counts are scattered. I have never heard of something like this before, and I have read countless case studies in medical journals."

"That's what happens when your energy is stolen," said a familiar, feminine voice from behind us.

We turned around and saw Dr. Gabrielle standing at the room's entrance. She entered the room and joined us. "It always looks like sudden anemia, followed by drops in glucose and hemoglobin. Although, the white blood cell count being so variant is a new one."

James showed the results to the doctor. "His neutrophils and lymphocytes are very low, but his eosinophils, basophils, and monocytes are high. It's as though his immune system is confused as to what it is fighting."

She squinted at the chart, looking perplexed. "Hmm, I don't know how to interpret this, to tell you the truth. And unfortunately, Steph is out of town. She contacted me after she got a message from you. I got your message right after that. What were the four of you thinking?"

James placed the medical report down. "I apologize. It's my fault."

She looked at him, shocked.

"No. It's my fault," I said. "Nick didn't want to go, and neither did Kelly. But I just had to get the Ark. I'm sorry. I just wanted to get this stupid power under control."

"Right now, I'm blaming all of you!" she said angrily. "You realize that your group can lose its leader? He could die! There probably wouldn't be anything Steph could do at this point even if she were here." I wished I could be mad at her…but I couldn't, because she was totally right.

"What do you propose we do?" asked Kelly with a shaky voice.

Dr. Gabrielle sighed. "Wait here. I'm going to make a phone call. Then you're going to tell me exactly what happened in perfect detail." She walked out of the room and forcefully closed the door.

"I wonder who she's calling?" I said.

James frowned. "Probably Kristiana, or Eli."

A moment later, the door opened back up. But it wasn't Dr. Gabrielle, or Dr. Bennett. It was a man in a hazmat suit that had letters emblazoned on his chest…

F.E.S.P.A.

# CHAPTER 7: F.E.S.P.A. RETURNS—ABBY

"Hello, children," the F.E.S.P.A. man said calmly. "My name is Dr. Charlitan. I've been put in charge of this hospital, and I must ask you a few questions."

We all looked at each other and took a step back. As we did, I felt a tickle in my nose and sneezed, and the doctor was Freeze-Framed.

When he unfroze, he looked at me warily. "Are you sick, young lady?"

"Me? No, it's just a cold," I answered.

He looked at me suspiciously. "I'm going to have to insist that you come with me."

"Um, No," I said, not even trying to hide the rebellion in my voice. "I'm staying right here."

He grabbed my arm. "It wasn't a request."

"Let go of me! I'm not going with you!" I yelled as I tried to free myself from his grip, but it tightened. "You're hurting me, let go!"

"What is going on here?" asked Dr. Gabrielle as she walked back into the room. Perfect timing.

"Step aside, miss," Dr. Charlitan said to her in a patronizing tone.

She raised an eyebrow. "It's doctor to you, my *good* sir."

He looked at her with disbelief. "Right, well, *doctor*, I'm afraid I have to insist that you move."

But Dr. Gabrielle wouldn't budge. "And I'm afraid I have to insist that you let go of that girl at once!" She took something out of her pocket and shoved it into Dr. Charlitan's face. It was her Edania Organization ID badge. "I am an administrator at the Edania Organization, and these four are under my charge. Now let her go, or things are about to get really ugly."

"Get that out of my face," said Dr. Charlitan in a condescending tone. "I'm taking this girl into quarantine. She's showing some symptoms of the mysterious illness that's going around. I would think that someone from the high and mighty Edania Organization would understand. Now step aside."

Dr. Gabrielle sighed. She touched my shoulder. "Excuse me, Abby. I'm going to have to borrow this for a second."

I looked at her, totally confused. "Borrow wha—"

Dr. Gabrielle aggressively pointed her finger at Dr. Charlitan, and he stopped moving.

"Unethical brute!" she said as she freed me from his grasp.

I couldn't believe what I just saw. "Did you… I mean…did you just—?"

"Freeze-Frame him?" she said like it wasn't a big deal. "Why, yes, I did."

"How?"

She smiled. "I simply borrowed your Segol. Well, not *borrowed* exactly. I'm able to copy the abilities of anyone I touch. Although, as you're about to see, it's not as strong as yours."

The F.E.S.P.A. doctor quickly unfroze. He turned around when he realized I wasn't in his clammy grip anymore. "Why, you!"

Dr. Gabrielle stood between me and him. "Nope, not happening."

He glared at her. "You meddling little—"

"Please, I dare you to finish that sentence," Dr. Gabrielle threatened.

"I'm getting my superior," he whined.

She laughed. "Yes, please do. Go on and run to the bossman, you foolish drone."

Dr. Charlitan stomped out of the room.

Dr. Gabrielle took a triumphant stance. "What a crybaby. Those F.E.S.P.A. goons only act big because they've got a lot of members. But get them alone and they're nothing but a bunch of toddlers."

"What are we going to do?" Kelly asked. "If he's going to get the same guy that we met last time, we're in trouble. He tried to kill us!"

Dr. Gabrielle looked at her. "You don't need to worry about that. What you *should* worry about is what I might do to you after you tell me exactly what happened when you decided to be a bunch of idiots and went to the waterpark unprepared."

There was a hush in the room.

"Come on, people!" Dr. Gabrielle said, tapping her foot. "It was a mistake. Own up to it and move on. What happened?"

We told her about breaking into Wacky Water World and trying to find the Ark, and that we found out how Wacky Water was causing people to get sick firsthand.

Dr. Gabrielle didn't blink the entire time. "Well, unfortunately…" She glanced over at Nick lying in the hospital bed. "You learned it the hard way. That said, it seems as though James was correct about this Corrupted controlling water. This gives us somewhat of a tactical advantage, if we play our cards right."

"One moment. You want us to go on the offensive now, at a time like this?" James asked, flabbergasted.

She nodded. "Yes, that is exactly what I'm saying. Obviously, the situation is much more dire than I had originally anticipated. First off, now that they know we're on to them, they're surely going to try something if we don't act. Second, Nick's stolen energy probably supplied enough power to either shatter the Ark's barrier completely or come dangerously close to it."

James lowered his head. "But our leader and strongest member is down."

"That he is, but we're going to have to deal," Dr. Gabrielle said, and her tone was actually gentle. "Besides." She smiled. "We have an ace in the hole."

James looked perplexed. "I don't know what that means."

"She's implying that we have a secret weapon," Kelly translated.

"Right you are, Kelly," Dr. Gabrielle said, nodding at her. "And it's you."

Kelly looked shocked. "M-me?"

"Yes, you. You can control electricity, can you not?" Dr. Gabrielle asked.

Kelly looked very uncomfortable. "Kinda, sorta, sometimes."

Dr. Gabrielle shrugged. "Well, electricity separates water particles. If this…woman, can get vaporized by a small explosion and can reassemble herself, perhaps a jolt of electricity will render her unable to do so, thus destroying her."

"Brilliant idea!" said James.

"Yeah, except for the fact that I can't always get it to work," Kelly said, looking even more uncomfortable.

"You're going to have to," said the doc as she pointed at my brother. "Do it for Nicklaus."

Kelly walked over to the bed and looked down at Nick's unconscious body. "Okay, I'll try," she said solemnly.

"Wonderful," Dr. Gabrielle said with a gratified expression. "Now all we need to do is get you and Abby out of here."

"What about me?" asked James.

"You need to stay here with Nicklaus," said Dr. Gabrielle.

James took a step forward. "B-but—"

"He's your best friend, is he not?" she asked. Dang…guilt-trip much?

James nodded. "Yes, of course he is, but I need to—"

"Stay here," she interrupted. "You've got more medical knowledge than half of the staff here. Keep your eye on the F.E.S.P.A. doctors. Don't allow them to do anything you deem suspicious."

James sighed. "I will." He turned to me and Kelly. "Please be careful."

I nodded and tried my best to give him an encouraging smile, but it was hard knowing that Nick was hanging on by a thread. "We will. You too, James. Please watch over my brother."

Kelly glanced at Nick one more time. "Yes, take good care of him. You know how mad he'd be if you slept on the job."

"I would never sleep on the job when my friend's life depended on it!" James answered, sounding offended.

Dr. Gabrielle motioned Kelly and me forward. "Alright, we need to get you two out of here."

"How?" I asked. "If you hadn't noticed, there're F.E.S.P.A. guys all over the place, and the hospital is blockaded."

She smiled slyly. "I'll show you. Come on."

I turned to Kelly. "I do *not* like the way she said that."

"Hurry up," Dr. Gabrielle said as she scurried out into the hallway.

Kelly and I followed behind her.

"Hurry up!" she repeated.

There were dozens of F.E.S.P.A. soldiers pacing the halls, all of them wearing hazmat suits with their insignia emblazoned on them.

I looked around. "Um, yeah. How are we going to get around all of these people? I know for a fact you can't Freeze-Frame them all, because I wouldn't be able to. So, what's your plan?"

She glanced up at the camera. "Well, first, I'm going to do *this*." She snapped her fingers, and all of the security cameras fried at the same time. "That's something I learned from Gideon."

"How's that going to help us with the goons in the suits?" asked Kelly.

She giggled. "Well, I picked up a lot of fun tricks when I visited Tel Aviv. The Edania Organization branch in the Middle East has a lot of fascinating Segols. For example, I got this one from a brilliant rabbi in Galeela." She held out both hands. "Take my hands, both of you."

Kelly and I looked at each other.

"Come on, we don't have all day," she said impatiently.

We reluctantly grabbed her hands. The second we did, we zipped through all of the F.E.S.P.A. agents completely unnoticed. We moved through the lobby of the E.R. and through the front door. I felt a little nauseous as I let go of her hand.

"Wh-what was that?" Kelly asked, holding her hand to her head.

Dr. Gabrielle looked perplexed. "I don't really know. He tried to explain it to me, but I couldn't quite grasp how it worked. I just know I've been dying for an excuse to try it out."

"Hey, the three of you, freeze!" yelled another F.E.S.P.A. lackey.

"Now what?" I asked.

"Can't we just…move through them like we did in there?" Kelly asked.

"Nope," said Dr. Gabrielle. "I used all of that ability up…but there is another one I can try. I got it from this lovely agent from Cairo." She cleared her throat.

About fifteen or so men were running toward us, and Dr. Gabrielle started to sing a beautiful tune.

"What are you doing?" I asked as panic threatened to squeeze my body. "You going to sing them to death?" Just as I said that, all of the men fell to the ground before they reached us. I looked around. "I was so just kidding… Are they really dead?"

She shrugged me off. "Don't be so dramatic. They aren't dead. They're sleeping. Just step over them, they'll be fine."

We walked over the sleeping horde of F.E.S.P.A. guys and made our way to the Mustang.

Kelly and I got in the car.

"Alright, remember the plan," said Dr. Gabrielle.

"What plan is that?" Kelly asked.

She smiled. "Zap that crazy water woman to high heaven, of course."

"Then what?" asked Kelly.

"Find the Ark," Dr. Gabrielle answered plainly.

Kelly took a deep breath. "You make it sound so simple."

"It is that simple… Well, I suppose it is a little easier said than done. But I believe in you," she said.

"Gee, knowing that really gives me confidence," I muttered.

"Just go," she said. "And be careful."

I turned on the car and drove out of the hospital parking lot. The sun was rising as the hospital disappeared from the rearview mirror. *Please, Nick. You've got to fight. You have to make it.*

***

Wacky Water World was packed as we drove into its parking lot. It was crazy nobody had connected the energy-draining water to the illnesses. Even if you *didn't* know that the water was some kind of freaky liquid made by a psychopath that slowly drained your energy, it seemed pretty obvious. I mean, the sickest people were the ones who drank the most of it. I'm sure that they even brought some with them to the hospital.

"Okay, so do you really have an actual plan?" I asked.

"Not really," Kelly answered. "What I do know is that we need to get to the factory area."

"Well, the aquatic freak knows who we are now," I said. "It's not going to be easy."

"She wouldn't attack us in public," Kelly said. "That would expose her as a Corrupted, and they don't want the world to know about them."

I shrugged. "True, but how are we going to get into the factory?"

She thought for a moment. "I don't know. I guess we'll have to improvise."

I rolled my eyes. "I think you've been hanging out with my brother way too much, and he's wearing off on you."

She frowned and looked down. "I just hope I'll be able to spend more time with him."

I touched her shoulder. "Hey, he's gonna push through this. And we're doing this for him, so let's go kick some butt."

She nodded. "You're right, we have to stay strong for him. Let's do this!"

We got out of the car and made our way to the park's entrance. The worker there blocked our way in. He was one of the meatheads that grabbed us when we had our little run-in with Marina. He wasn't even a real guy, either. He was made from Marina's water.

*Uh-oh, does he recognize us?*

"Hold up there, girls!" said the meathead.

Great, mission failed…

"It'll be thirty dollars to get in today," he said.

*Good, looks like he doesn't recognize us… Wait a minute.* "Thirty dollars?" I repeated.

He stood up straight, which made him look even bigger. "Yup, the grand opening celebration is over. So it's thirty dollars, or you're gonna have to beat it."

"I have a better idea," I said as I raised my hands. He and the other worker at the entrance froze in place. "Thirty dollars… Can you believe that, Kelly? They want us to pay thirty dollars! I'd rather not have to *pay* to get killed."

"Uh, Abby?" Kelly said, blinking at me.

"What?"

"Why'd you Freeze-Frame them?"

I walked through the entrance. "So I could do this."

"Are you crazy?" Kelly said, wide-eyed. "What about all the people who are walking around that you didn't freeze?"

I waved my hand. "Oh, like they would notice. Hurry up and come over here before they unfreeze."

Kelly nervously skidded through the entrance, and the two of us ran into the park.

"Wow, I can't believe that worked!" I said. "I guess I *am* getting the hang of it."

"We can celebrate later," she huffed. "Let's just go inside."

We walked into the indoor area of the park. There were people everywhere, having the time of their lives, not knowing that they were splashing in energy-draino water.

Kelly pointed toward the Tunnel of Love. "Look, the ride is out of order! There's probably nobody up there."

I sighed. "Every time we go up there, we get caught."

"Third time's the charm," she said as she started toward the stairs.

"Fine…" I said with as much enthusiasm as I could muster…which wasn't a lot.

We waited until nobody was around, ducked under the block-off gate and ran up the stairs.

The room was empty and quiet. But that didn't make me feel better. Marina could pop up out of nowhere and douse us with her Satan water. We walked over to the door. The floor was still soaking wet from the night before.

Kelly took a bobby pin out of her hair and started picking the lock.

"Hopefully people don't start shooting out of the floor like last time," I joked nervously.

"That's not even funny," Kelly said as the lock made a *click* sound. She opened the door and we looked inside. The coast was clear as far as we could tell, so we walked through the door and shut it behind us.

I was expecting to see a concrete floor and pipes overlaying the walls with steam blowing out of them. But we were in a narrow hallway with an expensive-looking tile floor and blue-tinted windows that overlooked the indoor part of the park on either side.

We cautiously walked down the hallway. I prepared myself for a creepy giggle and torrents of water any minute. But it was silent. I couldn't even hear the joyful screams of people below us enjoying themselves at the devil's waterpark.

There was an elevator at the end of the hallway. Kelly hit the up button, and the door opened.

"Hey, Kelly?" I said as she started to walk into the elevator.

She looked at me. "Hmm?"

"Do you remember that giant birdcage we were stuck in back at Hotel Barbaas?"

"Yes?" she said, confused.

I nodded. "Me too."

"What brought that up?"

"Just a feeling of déjà vu."

"Well, it doesn't look like a birdcage."

"Maybe that's what they want us to think."

"Come on!" she said as she hopped in.

"Fine, but if we get stuck in this elevator, I am so blaming you," I said as I hesitantly stepped inside the cab.

"Which floor do we want?" I asked. There were six.

"Let's aim for the top," Kelly answered as she hit the button for the sixth floor.

We reached the sixth floor and got out. It wasn't riddled with pipes or puddles of water or tetanus. In fact, it was a really nice office. A hallway led to a foyer with a stone reception desk with seashells carved into it, and a sign on the wall behind the desk said *Wacky Water World Management.*

An unseen force seemed to pull me forward. "Do you feel that?" I asked Kelly.

She nodded. "Yeah. The Ark is somewhere up here."

"What are the chances that it's just behind the reception desk?" I said hopefully. "We could snatch it and run."

She squinted at me. "Has it *ever* been that easy?"

I shrugged. "It could happen."

"Not to us," she said cynically. "Now, let's go."

We walked down the hall and into the foyer. There was a receptionist, and a few people in the waiting room area.

The receptionist was a young woman wearing a kimono similar to Marina's, only hers was bright orange. She looked over at us. "Excuse me, but do you have an appointment with Miss Marina?"

"Uhh," was all I could say.

Kelly jabbed my side. I looked at her, and she flicked her hands, mimicking how I use my Freeze-Frame.

"Are you kidding?" I whispered. "Do you see how big this office is? There's no way it'll work."

"You froze the guys at the entrance, and we were outside," she whispered back.

"That was at point-blank range, and there were two guys standing close together."

"We're close to the Ark," she pointed out. "Maybe close enough for you to get a power boost. Just give it a try."

The receptionist interrupted. "If you two don't have an appointment, you're going to have to leave."

Kelly nudged me. "Come on, hurry."

I glared at her.

The receptionist picked up her phone. "Alright, I'm calling security."

Kelly flipped the phone out of her hand with her gravity power. The receptionist bent down to pick it up.

"Hurry!" she said.

"Okay, fine! Don't rush me."

The receptionist sat back up, and continued to dial. I raised my hands to Freeze-Frame the room, but nothing happened.

"See?" I said.

"Try again," she said, like it was a simple request.

I concentrated as hard as I could.

"Hey, this is Myra up on the sixth floor, we've got a problem."

I flicked my hands.

Myra glared at me as she spoke on the phone. "There are two—" She stopped talking.

I looked around. She, along with everyone else in the room were frozen.

"Hey!" I said triumphantly. "I did it!"

Kelly smiled. "I knew that you could. How long do you think they'll be frozen for?"

I started to walk down the hall to the right of the reception desk. "I don't know, but not long."

Kelly joined me, and I could hear the receptionist say, "Where'd they go?"

We ran down the narrowing hallway. There was one door at the end of the hall. I opened it and we hurried inside. I turned and closed the door behind us.

"Great, now what do we do?" I asked.

"I don't know, but we made it this far, at least." *Way to find the silver lining, Kelly.*

We turned to look at the room, and my jaw dropped. It was gorgeous. The floor was tiled, and the ceiling was arched, with several marble pillars supporting it. A dome ceiling with deep blue stained glass sparkled above us.

There were three fountains in the room, two smaller ones to the left and right, and one big one in the middle that had a statue of a mermaid holding a jar in its center.

"Kelly, look!" I yelled as I pointed above the jar the mermaid was holding.

The Ark was hovering just above the fountain. It was struggling to float, and its color was dull.

I hopped into the fountain and climbed the statue. I grabbed the Ark, and it started to glow a brilliant sapphire blue. A flash of light blasted out of it and shot me backward into the water.

Kelly helped me up. "Are you okay?"

"Yeah…that was a rush! My whole body is tingling."

"Well, now we have it," she said. "I say we get out of here and regroup with the others at the hospital."

"I don't think so," said a muddled voice from the middle fountain.

The water in the fountain shot up and solidified into the shape of Marina. So much for an easy escape…

She giggled. "Ooh, aren't you two brave? Or, perhaps suicidal. I distinctly remember putting an end to your handsome friend's life. Are you so eager to join him in peaceful sleep?"

"Shut your trap, you witch!" I snapped.

She opened her mouth in offense. "Such vulgarity coming from such a young woman. Hmph, how unrefined. And you're stealing from me? Do you know how hard I worked to finally break the Ark's barrier? I just applied the final bit of energy not five minutes ago, and the two of you come barging in and try to take it from me? The nerve!" She held her hands out toward the two fountains to the right and left of her, and a giant bodybuilder made of water appeared out of both of them. "Snap them in half, my lovelies," Marina said joyfully.

The monstrous men leaped out of the fountains and ran toward us.

I lifted my hands and Freeze-Framed the room. "Well, look at that. I'm getting better control already."

We turned around to leave, but Marina appeared in front of the door with a splash of water. "You're not going anywhere."

We backed up. "Sh-she didn't freeze!" I yelled. I looked at her flunkies, who were still frozen in place. "They're frozen, but why isn't she?" Truth be told, I was more offended than scared.

Marina giggled. "I'm afraid I'm immune to your little party trick. You see, my body actually lies between two dimensions: this one, and one of my own design. Therefore, I'm constantly out of the range of your time freezing power, no matter how close I am to you."

"You…made a dimension?" said Kelly in disbelief.

She looked at Kelly with a warm smile, but her eyes were as cold as ice. "Why, yes. My Tide of Illusion allows me to make illusionary effects of such power that I can literally make my own world." Her smile curled into a wicked grin that matched her subzero eyes. "Would you like to go there? It's the best ride in Wacky Water World."

Kelly's hands began to glow with electrical power.

Marina lunged toward us and grabbed us both by the neck. The electricity in Kelly's hand faded. "No, there will be none of that," said Marina. "Time for you two to try the Wacky Water Tower. I do hope you enjoy the ride."

She pushed us both forward, and we were caught in a large jet of water and swept away in a rapid stream. I couldn't move, and I could hardly keep my head above the water. I couldn't see where we were going, but I could tell we weren't in the room with the fountains anymore. Suddenly, we were shot out of the darkness and started to fall fast. I looked down, and all I saw was a vast body of water hundreds of feet below.

We kept falling and falling…and it was a long way down.

# CHAPTER 8: WACKY WATER TOWER—ABBY

Down we fell, faster and faster. *How can we be falling this far? The water factory is only a few stories high. How are we falling from hundreds of feet in the air?*

I closed my eyes, bracing for some sort of life-ending impact. When we stopped, it wasn't the hard crash landing I was bracing myself for. I opened my eyes, and Kelly and I were floating above a vast body of water, hanging about a foot above it.

I opened my mouth to speak. "Wh-what is going—" Our bodies fell into the water. It was harshly cold. But it was worse than that…it felt like it was strangling the life out of me.

I popped my head out of the water. "Kelly?" I yelled.

Her head shot out of the water about five feet away. She spat water out of her mouth in a spray of mist. "I'm here!" she yelled.

I spun myself around, trying to see where we were. There was nothing but turquoise water below and a totally unreal, glassy, pale yellow sky above with a paper-thin layer of cloud that covered it.

I could feel the water against my skin. It wasn't normal water. It felt like it was stabbing at me, trying to seep its way into my skin, trying to drown me and drain my energy.

"We need to swim for it!" Kelly said, she was right next to me, urging me to swim. But where would we swim to?

She was right, though. We had to do something, otherwise we'd die right where we were floating. We swam as fast as we could, but it seemed as though we weren't moving forward, and it felt like the water was trying to pull me down. *Was this what Nick felt when he was thrown down that death slide? The water stabbing at him with its cold, unrelenting liquid daggers?* Ugh, that was a thought I wished I could drown out.

It was getting harder to breathe, and paddle, and move.

"What is that?" Kelly asked, looking forward.

I looked ahead. A giant shadow seemed to rise out of the depths. It looked like a building of some kind, surrounded by thick fog.

*Is it a lighthouse?* I thought. The building got closer and closer, even though we weren't paddling at all anymore. It was approaching so fast that I thought it was going to crash straight into us!

"Eep!" I squealed, waiting for the tall, spirelike building to bury us deep in the water. But the building stopped about thirty feet or so in front of us. Gleeful music was playing in the background, like the kind that played at Wacky Water World. It was that one song that always plays in amusement parks… "The Entertainer," I think it's called. It was muffled, though, like it was coming from underwater.

The fog cleared, and I could see the tower in front of us more clearly. It looked like some weird sci-fi version of a waterpark. It was hundreds of feet tall, and had waterslides popping out of the walls of every floor. A waterfall on the left side of the building started on the ground floor and flowed upward toward the sky. About halfway up the tower, stone balconies moved from one window to another. It reminded me of some kind of final level in a video game.

I suddenly felt something solid under the water as my knees and hands rubbed against it. Tile.

Now we were in about a foot and a half of water. I looked down. The tiled bottom of the small pool we were now in rippled a deep blue color.

"Okay, did we just trip out from some spiked pool water?" I asked, trying to get up. My body felt like it was made of lead.

Kelly stood up and started to wring out her long, dirty-blonde hair. "Something like that," she said. "Oh, that waterlogged witch is going to get it next time I see her. Look at my hair!"

I looked around us. On the far side of the small pool was an opening to the vast ocean we had just been helplessly splashing about in. In front of us were three marble steps that led out of the pool and into the strange tower's courtyard.

The water was still stabbing at me, stinging my skin as it trickled down. And it felt like I hadn't slept in days.

We stepped out of the pool. As soon as we did, we were completely dry. Looking up at the tower, I noticed that the first six or so stories strongly resembled the water factory and the the indoor area of Wacky Water World. The rest of the long, thin, spiraling tower shot out of the factory's roof.

The music stopped abruptly, and the familiar, totally annoying voice of Marina rang on the loudspeakers. "Welcome to the Wacky Water World Tower. You are now part of a very exclusive group of people who are privileged enough to behold its wonder."

Kelly looked around us, then up at the tower. "How are we going to get out of here?"

"You may wonder how you're going to get out of here…" Marina's voice answered from the speaker. "The answer is simple. Just make it to the tip-top of the tower in three hours. If you can do that, then you may exit the attraction. Be careful, though. There are many twists and turns within these walls, and who knows what kind of fun and exciting surprises you'll run into? Enjoy…"

"Ugh, I hate that sea hag!" yelled Kelly.

"Plus side?" I said. "At least we have the Ark." I went to fish it out of my pocket, but it wasn't there. I patted myself down. "Uh-oh."

"What now?" Kelly said.

"I can't find the Ark! What if I dropped it when we were in—" I turned around and looked back at the small pool that led out into the eerie sea.

"Well, we can't go back there," Kelly said, looking at the giant body of water with disdain. "Even if that's where it is."

Marina came back on the intercom. "Wacky Water World is not responsible for the loss of life, limb, or property, including cell phones, watches, wallets, jewelry, or Arks. Thank you and enjoy your stay at the Wacky Water Tower."

I sighed angrily. "That cheating little…"

Kelly walked toward the tower's entrance. "We need to focus on getting out of this place. Let's get started."

I rolled my eyes. "This is so going to be like the stupid tree-hotel, isn't it?"

The doors of the tower slowly slid open, just daring us to go in. When we stepped inside, the doors slammed behind us, and a pillar of water shot out of the floor and solidified into a wall, blocking the exit. *Well, looks like we can't go back.*

We were in a narrow hallway, and the walls looked like translucent blue glass, but they rippled like they were made of water. There was a muddled noise coming from behind the walls. It was hard to hear, though. Kelly looked through the watery-glass wall to the left side, and I looked through the wall on the right.

There were people on the other side of the wall! It was Wacky Water World. Now that I was closer, I could hear the music and the laughter and the screaming joy of the people on the rides, but it was very muffled, like I was twenty feet under water. People were walking right to me, but vanished from view at the last second, only to reappear on Kelly's side. We both banged on the walls as hard as we could.

"Help us!" we both yelled in unison.

Hitting the wall was like hitting a wet slab of concrete. Every time I pounded on it, it would send a ripple down the whole wall, but it didn't make a sound.

After a moment, parts of the see-through walls began to swell until there were four solid pillars of water on either side. The noise from the real world got so quiet, I had to strain to hear it. Kelly and I backed away from the walls and into each other. The pillars of water vanished, leaving us in a dark space.

Several dim lights turned on all around us, revealing a large room. It looked almost exactly like the foyer of Wacky Water World's indoor area, but it was a mirror image. Everything was reversed, and there was no entrance or exit from the building. The windows were tinted a deep blue, like we were submerged in the ocean. To the right was a sign that said *retaehT*. Red-carpeted stairs led to the structure. Straight ahead was a familiar archway with a sign above it that flickered a gloomy purple. *evoL fo lennuT*.

"The theater and Tunnel of Love," said Kelly. "The words are reversed just like the building… So, where should we go?"

"Not the theater, that's for sure!" I said desperately. "I really don't want to find out what's hiding in there."

"The Tunnel of Love, then?" said Kelly.

I shuddered. "I don't want to go up there, either. But if this *is* a mirror image of the stupid waterpark, the entrance to the factory is up there, and it looked like the factory leads to the tower."

We made our way to the arched entrance to the reversed Tunnel of Love. The checkered floor reflected the sign's purple glow, which reminded me of last night when we got ambushed by Marina.

I wondered what was waiting for us as we went up the stairs, but part of me really didn't want to know.

The room was much larger than the real Tunnel of Love. It still had the checkered tile floor and walls, but several portraits lined the walls, all of them portrayed those creepy animatronic characters, Princess Waterdrop and Wacky William, and all of them were staring at us. *Gross.*

This Tunnel of Love wasn't a slide. It was an actual cavernous tunnel that led up to the room by long, thin steps. There was a high archway between the cavern and the room we were in. Big, neon purple letters spelling Tunnel of Love backward buzzed and glowed eerily.

I looked at the wall where the door to the factory should've been. "Hey, Kelly?"

"Hmm?" She leaned closer to me, still keeping an eye on one of the portraits. The one right ahead of us was Princess Waterdrop. She was sitting on a plushy chair with her hands delicately folded on her lap. A portrait of Wacky William was to the right of the princess's. He was juggling about ten spiked balls, looking straight ahead with an obnoxious and evil grin. The whites of their eyes were glowing in the dark, slightly bulging out of their heads.

"The door isn't there…" I said. Where the door should have been was a large portrait of the princess and clown holding each other and staring at us, both bearing unnerving grins.

"Now what should we do?" she asked.

I shook my head. "I don't know, but I don't want to be in here for another second."

Static came from a speaker somewhere in the large, empty room. We both jumped.

The lights flickered a little brighter, and music started to play slowly while static hummed in the background.

"Welcome, welcome, to the Wacky Water Tower's Tunnel of Love," said a terrifyingly goofy voice. "Wacky William here, and this version of the classic ride is even more exciting than the original. Hop onto my own special boat: the *S.S. Waterdrop*, and venture through the tunnel's caverns. Some say that there is even a secret passage to the lovely princess's castle somewhere in there! See if you can find it." He let out an outlandish giggle.

"I hate this place!" I yelled as my whole body shivered.

Something moved in the darkness just beyond the mouth of the cavern, and it was coming toward us.. It was a boat. It docked itself right near the water's edge.

Kelly walked toward the cavern.

"What are you doing?" I yelled.

"Getting in the boat," she answered.

"Why?"

"So we can move forward. You wanna get out of here, don't you?"

I looked around, seeing all of the portraits of the jester and creepy princess glaring at me. "Absolutely!" I said as I joined her.

We stepped into the boat and sat down. The seats were cushy and almost comfortable, but they were cold and a little wet. The boat started its trek into the cold, dark cavern.

"This is totally a trap…" I said.

"It probably is," answered Kelly. "But where else are we gonna go, the theater?"

I shuddered. "No, thank you."

She pondered. "Now that I think of it, didn't we see the clown in the Tunnel of Love, too?"

"Stop thinking!" I said, not wanting to be reminded of it, and hoping that big-headed, hook-nosed, evil, grinning monster didn't pop out of the darkness. *Ugh, don't even think that, Abby!*

The boat slowed down, and the small lanterns that hung from the ceiling lit themselves and illuminated the cavern. I closed my eyes for a second, suddenly having flashbacks of the cave at Hotel Barbaas that held the poor people that the Illusion Tree's roots drained the life out of. I half-expected, and dreaded the thought of, lifeless bodies pinned to the walls and hands sticking out of the water. Luckily, when I opened my eyes, I saw nothing but the cave and water.

The boat drifted farther into the cavern, then turned right at a corner. Music started to play from somewhere ahead. The song itself was some classical composition, but the music was jingly, like it was coming from a jack-in-the-box.

The music steadily got louder as we rode through the narrowing cavern. A light came from a gaping hole in the cave wall that extended as far as I could see. I could hear the rushing of water as it spilled over into the room below. The gap was about halfway up the wall of the room, which had a sky-blue domed ceiling with clouds brush-stroked across it. In the center of the ceiling was a round light that was so bright it illuminated the entire room like a miniature sun.

More of the room came into view as we moved forward. A pool made of the cavern's stone covered about a quarter of the room, while the rest of the ground had green and lush synthetic turf. A yellow path with apple trees lining either side of it was cut in the turf.

The boat moved slowly down the spiraling track into the room, giving us a panoramic view as we descended. The closer we got to the bottom of the room, the more I noticed how surreal it looked. There were green hills painted on the walls, except for where the water was gushing from the opening in the cavern above. That part was made to look like a cliffside waterfall. On the section of wall that was hidden from view as we made our descent was a castle that touched the very top of the domed ceiling. It was very cartoonish, like it was from an old Disney movie. The boat slowly made its way around the perimeter of the room, and stopped at the waterfall pool.

"You did it!" Wacky William's high-pitched, obnoxious voice called from a speaker somewhere. "You found the castle of Princess Waterdrop!" He laughed clownishly. "Now get out and explore. You may find what you're looking for."

We stepped out of the boat onto the rubbery, fake grass.

"This place is ridiculous," I said. "It's like we're in a giant playhouse or something."

Kelly looked around. "I know. I just hope we can find the way out."

"Do you think that door to the castle is real?" I asked, squinting toward the tall structure.

"One way to find out," she said as we started up the yellow path through the lush fake greenery.

We made it to the castle's entrance. I touched the door, and that creepy music started up again. Suddenly, the bright light in the center of the ceiling went out.

Torches on the walls of the room lit themselves with bluish flames one by one.

We backed away from the door as the sound of an eerie wind crackled through the loudspeaker, followed by the recording of a crow's caw.

The plastic apple trees shook off their leaves, leaving their branches naked and jagged. Each tree had a caricatured, grinning face that began to glow yellow in the middle of their trunks.

Wacky William started to talk through the speaker again. "And now, the moment you've all been waiting for. Introducing the lovely, the wonderful, the enchanting…Princess Waterdrop!"

The castle doors creaked open, revealing a pitch-black space, and something was coming out of the darkness.

A life-sized animatronic doll wearing a purple and black gown clumsily wheeled itself out of the castle. It stopped, and its torso bent down, like it had broken its back. It slowly rose back into place, making a cringe-worthy rusty screech as it did. Its head was down, and its long, coarse, black hair hung down over the front of its body.

The doll's head slowly lifted with another rusty screech. Its eyes were sunken, and its pupils were up in its skull. Its fake, blue eyes started to roll all over the place like a chameleon's, then they shot forward and glared straight at us. Its mouth was like a marionette doll's, with two vertical lines that dropped from the lower lip to the chin.

"Hello," it said in a high-pitched voice as its lower lip moved up and down like a nutcracker's. "I am Princess Waterdrop. Welcome to my castle. I do hope you stay awhile."

I cringed. "Ew, not on your life, you Chuck E. Cheese reject!"

Princess Waterdrop's left eye twitched. "But—bu-ut, you must stay… This is the most joy-joy-joyous pla-ace in the whole wiiiide world!"

"Ugh, can we kill it now?" I insisted.

The anamatronic's eye kept twitching as it stared us down. Then, its head slowly rotated 360 degrees. "You musssst stayyyy," it hissed.

"Great, now we're fixing to be held hostage by Annabelle here," I said, backing away from the demon puppet. "As if this day could get any worse."

Princess Waterdrop's voice returned to its annoying high-pitch. "Oh, how naugh-ty. Naughty girls need to be taught a le-le-lesson!" The doll's mouth opened up wide, and needle-like teeth popped out from the top and bottom of its mouth. Razor-sharp claws extended out of its hands.

"Now I can see how you and Nick are related…" Kelly said, taking a step back. "You can't help but throw insults at the thing that's currently trying to kill us."

"Punish the naughty girls!" squealed the doll as it lunged toward us.

We dove out of the way but the doll managed to slash my right arm like butter. I crashed to the ground and clasped my arm. Luckily, the gash wasn't as deep as it felt. Kelly let out a scream as she crashed into one of the trees. She yelped as she held her left leg. Blood poured from the long, deep cut.

The doll licked the blood off of its claws with its robotic tongue and giggled. "Needs some su-su-sugar, this juice is a little bitt-er," it squawked.

It lunged for me again, and I somersaulted away from it, kicking it in the face. It let out an indignant scream and fell back two or three feet.

"How's that for sugar, Five Nights at Freddy's?" I yelled, trying to ignore the pain in my arm.

"Good kick!" yelled Kelly as she hobbled over to me.

The doll's head was bent backward so far that the back of its head touched its shoulders. A *zzzt* sound came from it as its head readjusted itself upright.

"Oh, my," it said. "This meat needs tennnnnnderized, or it won't be an-n-n-y gooood at-at-at the picnic with my-y-y Willie-pie!"

Its jaw unhinged, it opened its mouth wide like a snake's, and the needles receded back into its gumline.

Then came the buzzsaw. It popped out of the doll's mouth and turned on with a loud *VRRRRRM!* The doll lunged forward, and we just managed to keep ourselves from getting sawed open. Kelly and I ran as Bride of Chucky chased us with the buzzsaw hanging out of her mouth.

"Freeze-Frame it!" Kelly yelled from right next to me.

"I don't know if it'll work here!" I answered.

"Will it kill you to try?" she said, panting.

"It might!"

"We're dead if you don't! We're about to get sawed into pieces!"

"It's so-o-o-o fun playing tag with you!" the doll said in a creepily polite voice.

I turned around and held my hands out toward Princess Waterdrop, and the killer doll froze in the air midlunge.

"Now let's get out of here," said Kelly, gasping for breath.

The two of us ran toward the entrance of the castle. This area of the room wasn't frozen; the torches on either side of the castle door still flickered eerily. Kelly tried opening the door, but it was locked. She pulled a bobby pin that was still somehow in her hair after all of our falling, swimming and running around. She picked the lock and turned the knob. Something struck the door right above our heads. It was a dislodged nail from one of the princess's fingers. We turned around, and the doll stood there staring at us, the buzzsaw gone.

"Tag isn't o-o-o-over, dears, and there are no time-ime-ime outs!" the doll insisted.

"Abby, are you able to distract her?" Kelly asked all of a sudden.

I looked at her and raised my eyebrows. "You're kidding, right?"

"Can you?" she insisted.

"I mean, yeah, but why?"

She looked at her hands, then back at me. "Trust me. I just need a minute."

I sighed. "Fine, but you better not be thinking of ditching me!" I said, at least half-jokingly.

I ran in front of the demon doll debutante. "You have the worst aim I've ever seen! My half-blind friend can throw better than you."

The doll's eye twitched again, then it smiled. "Tag is one of my fav-fav-favorite games. Shall we resume? And this time, no-o-o cheating!" It opened its mouth wide again, and the buzzsaw came whirling out of its mouth and began to wheel itself toward me.

I ran around the room, almost tripping and falling into the pool of water. "Hurry up, Kelly!" I yelled as I passed the castle. My sliced arm was throbbing, but I kept running.

Kelly flailed her right hand. "I'm working on it! I just need a little longer!"

"What are you doing?" I said, running through the plastic meadow.

"Just keep running!" she yelled.

I glanced over my shoulder, and Princess Waterdrop was right behind me. The doll swung its buzzsaw. Before it laid into me, I leaped into the air and grabbed onto one of the plastic trees. The buzzsaw missed by just a few inches as I climbed up the tree.

The doll stopped at the tree and looked up, its neck screeching as it did. It giggled and sawed the tree in half. I fell on my butt and struggled to get up. All I could do was slide away.

"It looks like the games al-almost overrrr," said the doll.

"Hey!" Kelly yelled from the castle, her right hand surging with a golden glow.

Princess Waterdrop's head did a 180 and turned toward Kelly. "What is it, de-dear?"

"You're it!" Kelly yelled, and hurled a bolt of lightning at the doll, striking it right in its center.

Princess Waterdrop's robotic body buzzed and steamed and whirled around. Finally, the doll exploded with a *hissss*, sending several electrical pulses across the room in all directions. When the electricity struck the walls, the jolts travelled up and crashed against the ceiling. The entire room began to shake and rumble.

I hobbled over to Kelly, and we watched parts of the walls of the cavern tear apart like they were made of paper. The large cracks in the walls revealed the light and sounds of the real world. I could just barely hear people screaming with joy and laughter on the other side. The two of us ran to the crack closest to us. I could see the people splashing around in one of the indoor pools. I could hear the gleeful screams coming from the waterslides. I could even feel the air seeping through into this watery dimension. Kelly and I climbed up the wall and managed to get our hands through the crack before we were both shot back with a powerful blast of water.

We quickly got up and ran back toward the fissure, but before we could reach it, it repaired itself; first filling the gap with a torrent of water, then solidifying into the wall itself. We tried another crack, but it repaired itself as well.

As we looked around, all of the cracks in this hellish aquatic dimension sealed itself.

"I'm afraid it's not going to be that easy, ladies," said a calm voice from the waterfall pool.

Marina dove out of it like an evil water sprite. She took a few steps toward us. "My, my, my, I am impressed. You were able to create small breaches in my illusionary wonderland. I suppose I'll need to fortify it even more." She raised her hands, and the entire room was surrounded by a vortex of water that solidified into walls thicker than before. She sneered at us. "There. Now even if you manage to strike the first layer down, it will fix itself before you have a chance to break through the second."

We both stared at her with shock and hatred.

She calmly adjusted a strand of silky hair that was slightly out of place. "Remember the rules. I told you how to escape. You just need to reach the top of my tower before time runs out. And it looks like you have…" A large bubble appeared from the palm of her hand and changed into a clock. "An hour left. Better hurry." She cackled, then covered her mouth. "Oh, I do apologize, that was certainly not very ladylike. At any rate, I'll leave you to finish our little game. Ta-ta." With that, she vanished behind a pillar of water.

"An hour?" I said despairingly.

"We need to get going," Kelly answered.

We walked to the now destroyed castle. Despite the rest of the structure's massive damage, the front doors were perfectly intact. Kelly turned the knob. Suddenly, the floor opened up, and we fell through the hole like we were in an old Scooby-Doo episode.

We slid down a chute for what seemed like forever. It finally spat us out into a dark room, and we crashed onto the cold, hard, wooden floor.

Kelly got up. "Marina sure does make realistic illusions. Lord knows the bruise on my butt won't be an illusion in the morning."

"Let's hope we're alive to *see* the morning," I said. I looked around, and there was nothing but darkness. "*Now* where are we?"

We carefully walked forward. We knew we had to hurry, but we didn't want to run into any more nasty surprises. The room was almost pitch black, and it was nearly impossible to see anything in front of us.

I ran into something. It was soft and velvety…a curtain of some kind. Then it hit me like a splash of icy water, shocking and frigid. We must be in the…theater. No sooner did the thought cross my mind than the curtain rose. The blinding spotlight blared on the two of us.

"Kelly?" I said with a drop of fear in my voice, or several drops…or a torrential downpour.

"What?" she said, covering her face with her hand.

"We're in the theater…" I squeaked.

"Thank you," she said sarcastically. "I thought for a second that we might be in the souvenir shop."

The speakers turned on, but there was nothing but static on the other end.

I started to hyperventilate. "Okay…okay…" I said to myself between breaths. "It's gonna be okay…except you may be living your worst nightmare… Oh gosh…oh gosh…oh—"

I was interrupted by the loudspeaker. "Attention, ladies and gentlemen!" It was Wacky William. "The show is about to begin. Let's hear it for the lovely ladies who will be playing my victims tonight!"

A phantom crowd cheered and whistled. My eyes adjusted just enough to see there wasn't a soul in the audience.

"Kelly, I can't do this!" I said, barely able to utter the words.

She grabbed my arms. "Abby, we need to focus. We need to find our way to the top of the tower, remember?"

I closed my eyes and breathed for a moment. "...Okay."

Mad laughter came from stage right. I looked over and saw an animatronic Wacky William flipping and dancing its way toward us. The head, feet, and hands were slightly enlarged. Its face was more humanlike than Princess Waterdrop's, and it was painted ghost white. Its giant, hooked nose was red at the tip, its eyebrows looked carefully painted on, and its expression was of permanent surprise. Its red lips were smiling from ear to ear. Its eyes were large, bulging out like in the paintings in the Tunnel of Love room. The doll looked like an old-school cartoon jester, with a hideously happy grin and a red-and-yellow checkered jester hat and suit.

"Hello, there!" the animatronic said in a nauseatingly happy tone. It took its hat off and dramatically felt around for something in it. Its smile widened as it pulled a rusty handsaw out. "Do either of you wish to help me with my performance? I was thinking of sawing one of you in half!"

"I'm so out of here!" I yelled.

The two of us tried to run off stage, but the doll flipped its way to the stairs before we could reach them. Kelly and I jumped off the stage and started running up the aisles as Wacky William let out a mad cackle.

We reached the exit, but a gate suddenly fell over it, locking us in. The only door that wasn't gated in was along the right wall near the stage.

William laughed even harder. "These girls are a riot, aren't they, folks?"

The nonexistent crowd cheered and laughed. I felt like I was in the world's creepiest sitcom!

The animatronic jester leaped over the seats and landed right in front of us. It danced idiotically as the phantom crowd cheered it on. Then it stopped abruptly and rushed us, giggling like a lunatic. Kelly held her leg out and tripped the doll and it went sprawling. We ran for the door that wasn't blocked.

"I'm coming to get youuuuu!" Wacky William sang as it leaped over the chairs.

We opened the door and ran in, slamming and locking it behind us. The evil jester started to bang on the door. "You can't stay in forever, you know…" it chided. "Your public awaits!"

There was a narrow, flimsy-looking set of stairs in front of us with *CATWALK* painted on the fourth or fifth step. About halfway up the endless climb, I heard the door bust open.

"Olly olly oxenfreeeeee!" William yelled.

"Run faster!" I screamed.

Kelly and I ran up those stairs as fast as we could. We finally reached the catwalk. It looked like we were sixty feet off of the ground. The walkway was so narrow it felt like I was on a balance beam. We carefully made our way across it. Luckily, there were rails on either side to hold.

The entire catwalk shook, and Kelly and I both had to grab on to the rails to keep from falling. Behind us, Wacky William took hold of both rails and shook the catwalk, laughing crazily. Then it lunged up in the air, flipped above us and landed at the end of the catwalk in front of me.

"Time for your swan dive!" the doll said. It put its index and middle fingers on its mouth and curled its lips. "Oops, I meant swan song!"

"Freeze-Frame it, Abby," Kelly said.

I frantically flicked my hands quickly toward William, but it wasn't freezing. "I can't… I must be panicking *too* much for it to work!"

Wacky William hopped toward us, cackling madly as it drew near. It was shaking the catwalk as it approached, and it felt like we could fall at any minute.

# DOREN REPORT #6: ON DARK-SEGOLS— REALITY BENDERS

*TOLLES ISLAND*

*DEATHBORNE CAVE*

*FLUTURA'S LABORATORY*

Flutura paced the laboratory floor, muttering under her breath. After a moment, she returned to her computer and began to type, her eyes glued to the screen.

*Let's see if I can find anything on it here*, she thought, studying the screen. No results. She slammed her fist down on the table and grunted in frustration. There had to be *something* in Master Doren's database to help her.

Then, she remembered something that she overheard Thistle and Dr. Barbaas discussing. Something called the...

MALKIRIAN CIRCUS. She typed those words and hit Enter, hoping in her black heart that something would pop up.

SEARCHING... SEARCHING... SEARCHING... WARNING, FILES CORRUPTED. SHUTTING SYSTEM DOWN.

"The files were corrupted there, too?" she wailed, stomping her foot. "That is every archive in Master Doren's database. If I'm going to proceed to the next phase of my project, I need more information on—"

"Information on *what?*" a tranquil voice asked.

Flutura looked around her lab for the intruder. "You'd better have a good reason for trespassing into my laboratory," she said, grabbing a moth-shaped dagger from her belt. I hope you're ready to get gouged."

Water shot up from the floor and formed into Marina. She delicately placed her hands together like a princess and walked toward Flutura. "You really must be mindful not to speak with such vulgarity. You are a lady, and should act as such."

Flutura rolled her eyes and placed the blade back into her belt. "What do you want?"

"Oh, just stopping by," she said, smiling pleasantly. "I wanted to let you know that I have successfully imprisoned the two female Edanian agents *and* killed their leader. All that's left is the pale boy with the rather large glasses."

Flutura glanced at Marina with disbelief. "You…killed their leader?"

Marina giggled. "Yes, and two more are about to die. I am about to present the wonderful news to your master. Do you want me to include you in my telling of the tale? As I said, I have no interest in something as basic as glory. I'm simply here for beautiful vengeance."

Flutura gave a half-smile. "Vengeance isn't very ladylike, either."

Marina wagged her index finger. "Tsk, tsk, tsk. That is not entirely true. It all depends on how said vengeance is wrought, and I must say I have wrought my vengeance with the elegance of a true lady."

Flutura rolled her eyes. "Whatever you say."

"Do you want me to tell your master that you helped me with my mission or not?" Marina asked with a hint of impatience.

Flutura pondered for a moment. "Let's wait until we know the girls are dead, shall we?"

Marina frowned. "You don't think my water wonderland will ensnare them in its elegant grasp? Believe me, when they're caught in my watery web, they're as good as dead."

"I apologize," Flutura said insincerely. "I simply want to make absolutely sure they're all dead before we tell Master Doren. He's not one to forgive mistakes. Now, what about the Ark… Did you manage to collect it?"

Marina closed her eyes and sighed. "Well, yes and no."

"Which is it?"

"I had the barrier as good as broken, thanks to that uncouth but beautifully sculpted young man from the organization. He had so much energy, I was hardly able to contain it all. I didn't know one human could possess so much power."

Flutura tapped her foot. "So, where's the Ark?"

"Well, no sooner had the barrier been broken when those two roughneck little girls came and tried to snatch it." She exhaled angrily. "And they would have succeeded, if I hadn't stopped them. My minions are so inept!" she said angrily. She paused for a moment to compose herself. "At any rate, I sent those girls flying into my Wacky Water World Tower…along with the Ark. I haven't pinpointed the location of the Ark within my tower, but I know for certain that it's there. I just need to search the grounds and waters."

There was a moment of silence. Flutura cleared her throat. "Speaking of your tower…"

"What about it?" Marina asked haughtily.

There was another pause, but then Flutura blurted her question. "Is it a form of reality bending, or something different?"

"Hmph," Marina said, quickly looking away from Flutura and up at the ceiling. "Well, *that* sure is a personal question. But if you must know, it is indeed a form of reality bending."

"So, is it similar to what those of the Malkirian Circus could do?"

Marina took a step back and looked at Flutura in shock. "The…Malkirian Circus?"

"Yes, you've heard of it, haven't you?"

"Every Corrupted has heard of it," she said. She shrugged. "But I suppose I know more about it than most. Why such curiosity about them? When most of our kind hear the very name they tend to quake with fear."

Flutura glanced over at the chained-off wall with the thick, red curtain that obscured it. Then she glanced back at Marina. "I've been trying to research the processes of reality bending, among other things. It's part of a project I'm working on."

Marina peered at the blocked-off area of the lab. "What kind of project is that? You don't have a reality bending Dark-Segol, correct? What good is the information to you?"

"Just tell me what you know…please," said Flutura, trying not to sound impatient.

Marina stared at Flutura with a little unease, then took a deep breath. "Well, what I can tell you is…as powerful as my Tide of Illusion is, admittedly, it pales in comparison to the reality-warping Corrupted of the Circus."

"What do you know of its members?"

She shrugged. "More than most these days, but still not too much. The Circus is nothing more than a whisper among Corruptedkind now. I know that its four founding members were active even before the Edanian Civil War, and that Malkiria himself handpicked them to be his guards. This quartet of monstrous Corrupted became known as the Four Kings of the Malkirian Circus."

"What about the other members, not including the Four Kings?" Flutura asked, trying not to sound desperate for information.

Marina looked at her with curiosity. "What sort of experiment are you conducting again?"

Flutura sighed. "I can't say just yet," she said. "Please. What do you know about their powers and what became of them?"

Marina didn't answer for a moment. Then she folded her arms prim and properly. "I know that the Malkirian Circus was once an entire faction, about the size of the Olympian Alliance, and every Corrupted among their ranks had very powerful Dark-Segols, down to the foot soldiers. The single weakest link of the Circus was ranked higher than Doren, Pan, even Mistress Circe."

"They were that powerful?" Flutura asked, with both doubt and fascination.

Marina shrugged. "If the stories are to be believed."

"But Master Doren and the Olympian Alliance's leaders were the apprentices of—"

"I am well aware," Marina said. "But the Circus is…or rather, *was* on a whole different level than little old us. But we're here, and they're not, which I feel says something."

"What happened to them, exactly?"

"As the first war between Malkiria's army and the Edania Organization raged on, a majority of the Circus was wiped out one way or another. Most that remained alive were captured, but a few of their fates remain a mystery to both sides."

"Can you give me an example of one of those whose fate is unknown?"

Marina blinked. "I really don't see the relevance of this conversation."

"Humor me, please."

Marina sighed. "Very well, let me think of an example…"

"Well," said Flutura. "Let's just throw one out there… How about Bayoula?"

"The swamp woman?" Marina said in mild surprise.

"Just an example."

Marina raised one eyebrow, then glanced over at the chained-off curtain again. She started to walk to it, slowly and dramatically. "Such a strange interest, really," she said, caressing the velvety curtain. "Not many of us bother to study the Malkirian Circus. My sister and I did, but that was…out of necessity." She looked at Flutura and smiled. "Why, may I ask, are you so interested if you don't have a reality-bending Dark-Segol?"

Flutura quickly scuffled over to Marina, grabbed her arm and pulled it away from the curtain. "Like I told you, it's for a project."

Marina delicately took her hand back. "Hmm, sounds like an interesting project indeed, but let me give you a word of wa—" She stopped mid-sentence and her eyes narrowed into serpentine slits.

"What is it?" Flutura asked.

Marina's face was flushed and shocked for a brief moment, then it changed into a grim smile. "Oh, my. It would seem that my esteemed guests aren't playing well with my toys, and it looks like they're defacing my beautiful tower." She looked back at Flutura. "I apologize, but I must tend to this rude faux-pas."

"B-but I still have some questions," said Flutura.

Marina grabbed her arm. "Very well. I will drop you off in my office at Wacky Water World on my way to the tower, and we will continue the conversation there when I'm finished." Marina started to liquify.

Flutura saw her whole arm turning to liquid. She gasped. "Wait—"

Marina managed to smile before her face completely turned into water. "Don't worry, this is a very safe and efficient mode of transportation," she said, her voice echoing.

Flutura's entire body liquified into a pillar of crystal-clear water, and they both splashed out of sight.

Flutura's whole being shook and rattled as every cell in her body splashed around in the vortex of water. It felt to her like she would soon fall apart, to merge with this swift and rapid trail of water forever. But, at last, she felt her body shoot out of the ground and solidify again. She stumbled and fell to the floor. But it wasn't the floor of her lab. It was the floor of Marina's office in the Wacky Water factory.

Marina knelt down. "It is a bit of a head rush at first, but you'll soon be on your feet. I'll be back in just a moment." Marina vanished again with a splash of water.

Flutura slowly got up. She closed her eyes and put her hand on her forehead. After a moment, the room stopped spinning. She opened her eyes and looked around. A giant window that overlooked the waterpark covered the outside wall. There were shelves on the right and left sides of the room. The shelf on the left had two porcelain dolls. One was a princess with a blue dress and bulging eyes. The other was a jester with a red-and-yellow checkered outfit and belled-hat. A stuffed plushy of a blue, Chinese-inspired dragon coiled around them.

The shelf on the right had four porcelain dolls sitting on top of it that looked just like Marina. Each wore a kimono that had a very slight variation of blue. On the ceiling was a small fountain with a mermaid on the top of it, or, in this case, the bottom. The fountain was hanging upside down, but the water that shot from the mermaid's pot wasn't falling to the floor. Instead, it trickled upward into the fountain's upside-down pool. Water poured from the pool and onto the ceiling, where about two inches of water hovered right below it.

After a few minutes of snooping around the office, Flutura sat down on the aquamarine couch in front of Marina's desk.

*Reality bending…* Flutura thought. *Just how useful is it? How can I use it to acquire the remaining Arks? What kind of reality-warping ability does* she *have, and does it still even work after they—*

A jet of water shot out of the floor right in front of Flutura, and she leaped off of the couch just as the water solidified into Marina.

"You really need to stop doing that!" Flutura huffed.

Marina giggled. "It's just so much fun!"

"For you maybe, but you're going to give me a heart attack!"

"Don't be so dramatic," Marina said, flicking her jet-black hair. "Anyway, what were we talking about?"

"The Malkirian Circus and reality bending."

"Ah, yes. About that…" Marina stopped and seemed to ponder something. "I would take extra care."

"What do you mean?" Flutura asked.

"This *project* of yours," Marina answered. "Let me tell you this. All of the members of the Circus, every last one of them, cared very little about loyalty to anything except for absolute destruction. They made the rest of us look as moral as a…" Marina stopped and gagged, delicately covering her mouth. She composed herself, quickly returning to perfect posture. "…church choir."

"I don't… I mean, I'm not… I have no idea why you're talking about," Flutura stuttered.

Marina winked at her. "No, I don't imagine you do. But let me just think aloud for a moment. Even the low-ranked rabble of the Circus, such as the swamp woman, would think nothing of Corrupted as low on the food chain as you and me."

"We're not low on the food chain," Flutura said indignantly. "There are plenty of Corrupted ranked lower than us."

Marina waved her hand dismissively. "Yes, yes, I know. But, to the Circus, we would all be grouped together because we're of a lower rank than they. They would even show Doren or Mistress Circe great disrespect. So, I would not go there if it were me."

There was a long pause.

"The swamp woman," said Marina. "An interesting creature to use as an example. Why did you pick her? Why not Qayin the spear, or Philista the parasite, or even Isavel the desolator?"

Flutura shrugged innocently. "She was just the first to pop into my head. In truth I don't really know many of the others…except for Philista and Isavel. It's just Bayoula is one that—"

"She's one of the most obscure of all of them," Marina interjected. "Most Corrupted, even the ones who know of the Malkirian Circus as more than a pretty story, don't know her name. Out of the entire Circus, she had the weakest reality-warping Dark-Segol, you know?"

"She did?" Flutura said, trying to hide a great deal of disappointment.

Marina nodded. "Master Faust said that my Tide of Illusion is more powerful than her reality warping power…I think it was called the Mire of Nightmare or something like that. He said that her ability was even weaker than Ivy's Forest of Illusion."

"That…that is an interesting bit of information," she said glumly.

Marina noticed the deep frown on Flutura's face. "Why so blue? It's not *your* Dark-Segol's power that has come into question. Anyway, Bayoula the Swamp Woman compensated for her limited reality-shifting ability with a few other tricks."

Flutura looked up, her frown quickly dissipating into a look of intrigue. "Like what?"

"What she lacked in reality-bending efficacy, she made up for in brute strength. She was the most physically strong of the entire Circus. She was very swift despite her rather…robust appearance. She also had the interesting ability to become invisible. She was far from a pushover. They say that she was the Azusa family's greatest enemy."

"Interesting," Flutura said.

"Not really," Marina said, sounding bored. "If you really want to know the full potential the Circus had, you really should do a project on the Four Kings."

"Perhaps some other time," said Flutura. "Thank you for the

information."

"It was my pleasure," Marina said with a curtsey. "Now, on to other business. I hope that you're not too bitter about me taking charge of this mission. You don't have to worry about any other interference from me after this. Once this job is done, I will take my leave. Then you can go on an energy-stealing, Ark-gathering rampage… Just do me a favor and do so like a lady."

Flutura smiled. "You know, you're much more agreeable than your sister. I could almost tolerate you."

"My sister was pretty difficult to—" Marina stopped abruptly and gasped. It was a guttural, enraged sound. "Wha-what is the meaning of this?" Her eyes became sharp and predatory like a cat about to pounce. "Intruders… How?" she cried in a fury. Her well-manicured nails sharpened to jagged points. Her long, silky hair began to flow wildly upward like she was underwater. Her voice got hoarse and gurgly. "In *my* tower? How could this be? Nobody can just waltz into my domain!"

The water on the ceiling started to boil and, as though the water gates of heaven broke open, started to rain down from the ceiling. Then water began to pour in from all over the place. Torrents gushed from the walls and floor. In a matter of seconds, the two of them were knee-deep in water.

The water burned Flutura's flesh. She could feel the stinging of every droplet as they made contact with her fair skin. She jumped up on the desk, but the water continued to burn her. She grabbed a small pod from her coat pocket and threw it in the air. A blue, moth-shaped barrier six feet across shot out of it right above her. The indoor rain fell upon the energy-barrier and fizzled and popped out of existence, as if the water droplets were little embers popping out of a blazing fire.

Marina glared over at Flutura, her voice still hoarse. "If you will excuse me…there are some uninvited guests I need to drown. This game is over!"

She raised her arms up, and every drop of water in the room surrounded her. With a roaring *WOOOSH*, both she and the water vanished in a giant splash.

Flutura was breathing heavily. She snapped her fingers, and the barrier popped back into the little capsule. She caught it and put it back into her pocket. *And they say I have anger issues.* She hopped off of the desk.

The room was in disarray. The upside-down fountain was cracked, and the mermaid suddenly fell to the ground with a loud *CRASH!*

*I'm out of here*, Flutura thought. *And this time, I will use my own mode of transportation. It's much less nauseating.*

With one final look around the waterlogged room, Flutura morphed into several glowing moths, and they all flew out of the room.

# CHAPTER 9: BROTHERS—JAMES

It had been twenty minutes since the girls left, yet it seemed like an eternity. I paced, looked at the clock, at Nick, then at the heart monitor, and repeated the process. I really wanted to sit down, but the idea of sitting on a hospital chair sent me into panic mode.

I stopped pacing for a moment and took a closer look at the monitor, then down at Nick. His skin was very pale, and his lips were cyanotic and dry. His entire body was shivering, his heart rate was slow, and his breaths were swift and shallow. All of this pointed toward hypothermia. However, his temperature was 99 degrees. How could his body be going hypothermic when his temperature was on the upper range of average? It didn't make any sense.

I heard Dr. Gabrielle pacing up and down the hallway, talking to someone on the phone. "This is a mess, I tell you." There was a pause. "Yes, I would call this an emergency! Nicklaus is down and out, and who knows how the girls are going to fare?" There was another pause. "Just tell someone. Anyone. We have a situation here." She walked into the room, holding her phone up to her ear with a death grip. Her lips were thin and her face was an angry shade of red. "Just do it, that's an order!" She angrily hit the end button and shoved the phone into her pocket.

"Were the girls able to leave?" I asked.

Her face cooled, and her expression went from angry to concerned. "Yes, they were able to leave. How's he doing?" She walked over to me.

I looked at Nick. "About the same…" I said with an obvious crack in my voice.

She touched my shoulder. "He'll get through this."

I pulled away. "That is wishful thinking…medically speaking, his chances are—" I couldn't finish my sentence. I dared not use the word *slim* out loud.

"You need to realize something, James," she said, not unkindly. I didn't answer. "Look at me," she said firmly but gently.

I looked toward her, but could not meet her eyes.

She stomped her foot. "I said look at me!"

I finally made eye contact with her. She was quite intimidating despite being of such small stature, but her eyes looked warm and caring, at least at the moment.

She nodded. "You know science and are well-versed in reason and logic. But there is something you've got to realize about the human spirit."

"The human…spirit?" I repeated.

She smiled and nodded. "It can be a frail thing at times, but it can also be stronger than anything on this earth. And Nick's spirit…" She nodded toward him. "He's got the strongest one around. That's why Eli chose him, you know? For his courage and greatness of soul."

*Do I believe in the human spirit?* I thought to myself. *I suppose I do, deep down. If the soul indeed exists, Nick's would be strong. But is it strong enough to pull him through this?*

She stomped her foot again. "This is *not* a matter of intellect. Get out of your head." She poked me in the chest. "This is a matter of heart. Now, I have a job for you."

"For me?" I asked nervously.

She nodded. "Yes. I want you to check on the other patients, the ones who have similar symptoms as Nicklaus, the ones who OD'd on Wacky

Water."

"B-but I—" I looked back to Nick. "I'm supposed to be here for him."

"I can hold down the fort," she said. "Go. And be careful of F.E.S.P.A. Many of them are…taking a break right now." She chortled. "But they should be waking up soon."

*Waking up?*

"Go," she said, swatting her hand toward the door in a shooing gesture. "And be quick. I expect a status report when you return."

I hesitantly made my way to the hall.

"Please wake up, Nick," I whispered to myself as I thought back to a conversation we'd had three days before.

*"How can you claim such a thing? It is hardly rational."* My voice echoed in my head.

*"C'mon, J-Man. Things like this don't have to be rational,"* I heard Nick's cheerful, ghostly voice answer back.

I shook the thought away. *I can't think about that now… I need to focus.*

There wasn't a soul in the hallway. No doctors. No nurses. No one from the so-called Force-Pointe Emergency Situation Protocol Association. Were the F.E.S.P.A. grunts really on a break? Or, what seemed more likely, did Dr. Gabrielle do something to them? She seemed to be the sort to punch first, ask questions later.

I walked down the eerily quiet hall. I stopped and looked in one of the rooms. There were two kids in there, and I recognized one of them from school, Billy O'Neill. I was about to enter the room, but stopped. I would really get into trouble if someone walked in and saw me examining the patients. I was not a doctor. Plus, proper protocol would be to wear some personal protective equipment, just in case someone truly did have an infectious disease. Oh, what to do?

I took a deep breath. *I suppose I can try to use my Scan ability.*

I focused on the heart monitor, and my vision started to zoom in on it like it was a smartphone camera. It was working! A target cursor surrounded the monitor, and the Edania Organization computer's voice spoke in my head.

PATIENT'S NAME: BILLY O'NEILL

HEART RATE: 38BPM

TEMPERATURE: 94.3 DEGREES F

BP: 71/55

I looked over at the chart and Scanned it.

PATIENT HAS TYPICAL SYMPTOMS OF MODERATE TO SEVERE HYPOTHERMIA AND ANEMIA. TEMP AND HEART RATE LOW. BREATHING IS RAPID AND SHALLOW. SKIN IS CYANOTIC AND COLD TO THE TOUCH. PATIENT ARRIVED UNCONSCIOUS.

I used my Scan ability on the other patient's chart. It said roughly the same thing, although he was conscious when he came in, but slipped into unconsciousness soon after.

I went to the next room, and the next, and the next. I ended up going all the way down the hall. Out of the sixteen people hospitalized on this floor, only two of whom were adults, all of them were unconscious, and eleven of them were considered in critical condition. This Wacky Water epidemic was a terror. Though, I had to wonder if the poor conditions of Marina's victims were intentional. I knew Nick's was. Though, if Marina had her way, he would be dead. But everyone else? Perhaps she made the energy-draining water too addicting for its own good. This would surely draw attention to her eventually, something that the Corrupted try to avoid. Sure, it would allow her to gather more energy in a short amount of time, but Marina seemed too clever to take such a risk on purpose.

I made my way back to Nick's room, and I could hear Dr. Gabrielle raising her voice again

"Absolutely not!" she yelled.

I rushed in the room to see what was going on. There were four men in hazmat suits surrounding Nick's bed, and it looked like they were getting ready to move him.

"This boy is sixteen, meaning he is still legally a minor. You do *not* have parental consent, and you will *not* move him!" Dr. Gabrielle snapped.

Dr. Charlitan was the one taking the brunt of her anger. He held up his hands and said "Miss—"

"Doctor!" she interrupted. "I told you before, my name is Dr. Gabrielle."

He rolled his eyes. "Yes, well, *doctor,* you are not an M.D. Therefore, you have no idea what you're talking about. We need to take this boy down to the medical lab area. We're just going to run some tests on him. He's showing some slightly different symptoms than the others, and he's the most serious case."

"You must be deaf," Dr. Gabrielle retorted, her nostrils flaring. "I said *no!* He is an intern at the Edania Organization, and I am one of the administrators, meaning I am responsible for him. I absolutely forbid it! You F.E.S.P.A. fools are always up to no good. I know the kind of unethical tests you would want to run… They'd certainly be painful and potentially crippling."

The F.E.S.P.A. doctor leaned in and spoke into Dr. Gabrielle's ear. "Listen to me, you puny little Edanian puppet. I'm taking this boy, and you can't do a thing. We basically have martial-law authority here, so step off."

As this was going on, the conversation Nick and I had rang through my head again.

*"Why do you keep standing up for me?"* I asked him that day.

*"J-Man, that is the stupidest question that I've ever heard. Isn't it obvious?"*

I snapped out of it. I had to do something. "Hey!" I yelled as loud as I could, startling even myself.

Everyone looked over at me. I could feel my face turn red, but I could not let my anxiety deter me from saving my friend. I closed my eyes. "You are not taking him!"

Dr. Charlitan glared at me. "Tch, what are you going to do about it, boy?"

*If the soul exists, if greatness of soul is a factual concept…please, Nick, give me some of your courage.* I took a deep breath. "Wh-whatever is necessary," I answered as boldly as I could.

He stormed over to me. "You realize that you're interrupting a government investigation? You can go to prison for a long, long time."

"I…" I could feel my heart pounding out of my chest. But I thought back to my conversation with Nick again. "I don't care. I *won't* let you take him. Not without a fight!"

Dr. Charlitan shoved me hard, and I fell to the floor.

"James!" Dr. Gabrielle cried as she ran to me. "Oh, you are *so* not going to get away with this!" she yelled at the F.E.S.P.A. doctor.

He laughed. "Sure I will. We got away with our mantis extermination project without a hitch. It's for the good of the people, *doctor.*"

Dr. Gabrielle got to her feet and stared at him. She was a good two feet shorter than him, but she did not back down.

"Excuse me, Dr. Charlitan?" said a voice from behind me. It was Dr. Bennett, the head doctor of the hospital and the clinician who'd first looked at Nick.

"What do you want?" Dr. Charlitan asked impatiently.

Dr. Bennett looked down at me, then back at Dr. Troglodyte. "Is everything okay?"

"Everything is great," Dr. Charlitan said in a soft voice. "We're just trying to move this patient down to the lab area so we can run some tests."

"Well, that's going to have to wait," Dr. Bennett said, crossing his arms.

"There's a gentleman here, says his name is General Southland? He's asking that every member of your team come to the front immediately."

Dr. Charlitan stared at him for a long time, then turned to his cohorts. "Let's go, men." He looked back at Dr. Gabrielle with a heated glare. "We'll be back for him later…" he said, then he and the other F.E.S.P.A. ruffians walked out of the room.

"Are you sure everything is okay?" asked Dr. Bennett.

"Everything is fine…" said Dr. Gabrielle, trying to be calm. "Now, if you'll excuse me, I must make another phone call." She walked out of the hospital room.

Dr. Bennett looked at me with concern. "Are you going to be okay, son?"

I got up and brushed myself off, trying not to think about the fact that I was just on the hospital floor. I nodded. "I'll be okay."

He looked at me with disbelief. "Okay, just call if you need anything."

I nodded again and tried to smile, and Dr. Bennett walked out of the room.

I sighed loudly. *Now what are we going to do?* I thought. *What is going to happen if the F.E.S.P.A. grunts come back?*

I looked at Nick lying in his hospital bed.

*"We've been through a lot together…"* I heard him say in my head.

I took a step toward his bed. "I'm sorry, Nick. I'm not strong enough. If only things were reversed, then maybe something could be done to stop these F.E.S.P.A. guys. I don't know what I'll do if they come back in."

The heart monitor started to blare loudly. *Beep… Beep… Beep… Beep!*

As I looked at it, his heart rate started to go more erratic. *Beep, beep, beep, beep!*

His heartbeat was too slow just a moment ago, and now it was beating so fast he'd soon go into cardiac arrest.

His heart started to beat even faster. *Beepbeepbeepbeep!* It was 240 BPM, which was dangerously fast!

Nick started to thrash in his bed, his arms and legs flailing around. He was having a seizure! I quickly tilted his head to the side as saliva poured out of his mouth. His face was hot and wet.

"Help!" I yelled. "Dr. Bennett!"

I looked at the monitor again. His temperature was rising fast, skyrocketing to 105. His heartbeat was irregular and rapid.

"Dr. Bennett!" I yelled again.

Dr. Bennett ran into the room. When he saw Nick, he quickly called for the nurses, and four of them rushed in.

"Move, son," he said calmly.

I moved out of the way as the doctor told one of the nurses to get the diazepam, an antiseizure drug. She left the room and came back a moment later.

Dr. Bennett drew the diazepam up in a syringe and injected it into Nick's IV, and he quickly started to calm. After thirty seconds, he was motionless on the bed, but his heart rate was still erratic.

"We need to move him to the cardiac wing immediately!" said Dr. Bennett.

One of the nurses nodded and got on the phone.

A moment later, four men rushed in with a gurney. They moved Nick from the bed to the gurney.

They quickly carried him, along with the heart monitor and IV line, out of the room. I stood there in shock for a moment, then ran after them. When I reached the elevator, it was closing. I looked at the sign near the elevator.

Cardiac Wing: 4th floor.

I ran up the stairs to the fourth floor and scrambled across the cardiac wing lobby, where I saw them carting Nick through the large double doors.

Dr. Bennett stopped me. "Sorry, son, you can't come back here."

"Why not?" I asked.

"Family only beyond this point," he said.

The conversation suddenly rang into my mind again. "I am…" I said quietly.

"What?" Dr. Bennett said.

The entire conversation deluged into my mind. I had been trying to ignore it, but the floodgates broke.

***

Just three days before all of this foolishness, Nick and I were in the gymnasium after school. He had just scared off the Hyena Gang again because they were harassing me. When they were a safe distance away, Max Cassedy told Nick that he would "get what's coming to him."

Several minutes passed as Nick was blasting hoops or however you say it.

"Nick, why do you keep standing up for me?" I asked him abruptly.

He slipped and accidentally threw the ball into the bleachers. He turned to me with a frown that looked confused, hurt, and almost angry. "J-Man, that is the stupidest question that I've ever heard. Isn't it obvious?"

"I-I'm sorry…" I said, thinking I had just offended him. "I just don't want you to get hurt because of me. I mean, I know we're best friends, but—"

Nick took a deep breath and walked over to me. He plopped down next to me and slapped my shoulder. "You're more than just my best friend, J-Man. You're my brother!"

I frowned. "You mean…oh, how do they say it? Something like 'sibling from another parental unit'?"

Nick chuckled. "It's brother from another mother."

"Yes, that's it…"

"Well, that's what you are," he said cheerfully. "My brother!"

I looked at the floor. "How can you claim such a thing? It is hardly rational."

"C'mon, J-Man. Things like this don't have to be rational," he said with a grin.

"We haven't even known each other for three whole months yet, and you claim that you see me as your brother?"

Nick pondered for a moment. "It's not about how long we've known each other. We've been through a lot in such a short time. And through all that, we became brothers."

"But…what's the difference between you calling me your best friend and calling me your brother? It is simply another title."

"No, it isn't!" he insisted. "Agree with it or not, J-Man, you're family, and I'd take a bullet for family."

I didn't answer him back. I just changed the subject.

***

"I'd take a bullet for family," I whispered to myself as I stood before Doctor Bennett.

"Are you feeling okay, son?" he, asked.

"I *am* family," I blurted out. "I'm his…b-brother."

He looked at me, his eyes almost looked disciplinary. "You are? His twin sister didn't say so."

"I am his brother as surely as I am wearing these glasses, doctor," I said with every ounce of conviction I could muster.

He smiled. "Very well." He put his hand on my shoulder. "When we have him stabilized, I will come back to get you."

"Thank you," I said.

He rushed through the double doors.

*Brothers…* I thought to myself. *I think I'm finally starting to get it. I just hope I didn't realize it too late.*

Half an hour passed, and I was by myself in the lobby. I tried calling Abby and Kelly ten times to tell them what was going on, but the calls wouldn't go through. *I sure hope you two are doing better than we are.*

Dr. Bennett walked through the doors and slowly made his way toward me.

"How is he, doctor?" I asked him, but based on his frown I knew I was not going to like the answer.

He shook his head.

"Tell me," I insisted.

"He's…not doing well," he said solemnly.

There was a dreadful and empty silence for a moment, then I quietly asked, "What do you mean?" but I already had an idea.

"We tried to stabilize him. However, he is suffering from a very high fever. Truth be told, your friend…" He frowned all the more. "Or rather, your brother, may very well die, and soon."

My body felt numb. Was I really about to lose my best friend…my brother?

"Where did the girls go?" the doctor asked. "They should also say her goodbyes."

My mind felt almost as numb as my body. "They're…unavailable right now."

"I see," the doctor said. "Well, he should have someone in there with him. Come with me."

I just stood there. I found it nearly impossible to move. *This is some kind of nightmare. It has to be.*

I couldn't let myself just stand there. Nick needed someone to be there for him, so I forced myself forward and followed Dr. Bennett through the double doors. Everything felt like it was in slow motion, more evidence that this was simply a nightmare.

We walked down the excruciatingly long hallway and turned right at the end of it. There were two rooms on either side of this much smaller hallway.

Dr. Bennett opened the door of the first room on the left and motioned me to go in.

My throat was dry and painful. I tried to swallow, but I could not produce any saliva.

I walked into the room, and the doctor shut the door. It was dim; the lights had been turned down. It was a larger hospital room, and the bed was on the far end. The curtain was hiding most of the bed from view. I slowly made my way to the curtain. I grabbed it, but my hand almost slipped, because my whole body was shaking like I was the one who had the seizure. I slowly moved the curtain back to see my…brother, in a very pitiable condition. He looked like a human science experiment. There were several electrodes attached to his chest and stomach, and he was hooked up to an oxygen tank. His chest barely rose when he breathed. His whole body was drenched in sweat, and his closed eyes looked sunken in. He looked like a victim from one of those outbreak documentaries I love so much.

I glanced up at his heart monitor. His temperature was 107!

"Ni—" I started to say, but stopped. I closed my eyes as they started to sting and water. I took my glasses off and placed them on the little table next to the bed. "Nick. I-I'm sorry. This is all my fault. I should never have suggested that we even go near that place without a proper plan. I know Abby says it's her fault, but I know you look to me for sound advice. I messed up. I hope you can forgive me."

He was as still as the grave, barely breathing. His heartrate had dropped; now it was too slow.

"I truly wish things were reversed," I continued. "I wish I was the one in the coma. It's what I deserve. The team needs you, you know? You're the leader."

His heartrate slowed even more.

My eyes started to sting again, and my vision got blurrier than usual.

"You…can't leave me all alone. You were the first real friend that I've ever had, aside from Kelly. I can't imagine life without my best friend…"

All I could hear was the breathing machine supplying him with oxygen. Tears started to trickle down my face. I felt my legs buckle and give out. I fell to my knees on the side of the bed. I reached for his hand and grabbed it. His hand was hot and clammy.

"Please, come back," I blubbered. "If you do, I promise I will try harder not to mess up the colloquialisms of modern society, and I will go with you and Kelly and Abby to more sports events… I'll even try out for basketball next year like you wanted me to."

There was no response, save the hiss of the oxygen machine.

I put my face on the bed, and the tears rushed out even faster. "I never got to tell you, but you're my brother, too! I didn't realize what that meant until now…but you're my brother, Nick! I would take a bullet for you, too. I would even go through a tuberculosis ward if I had to, if it meant that you could come back!"

The air in the room suddenly shifted, and I sensed a presence watching me. Who, or whatever it was, felt familiar. I hoped to God it wasn't anyone from F.E.S.P.A.

I reached for my glasses with my free hand. Right when I grabbed it, Nick suddenly squeezed my other hand. I was so startled, I dropped my glasses.

"Sh-shake on it?" Nick whispered with an exhausted voice. He weakly shook my hand. "Now it's official," he said. "We're brothers."

I let go, grabbed my glasses from the floor, and put them on, not caring that they had just been on the ground. I stared at him, not believing what I was seeing. He was awake!

He grabbed the oxygen mask and took it off.

"You're…you're alive!" I said, gleefully.

He chuckled. "It's gonna take a whole lot more than a splash of water to get rid of me!" His voice was now full and healthy, but his face still looked flushed and tired. "So," he said, grinning at me slyly. "I guess this means you're gonna have to try out for basketball next year, huh?"

My face felt hot. I didn't think he actually heard me say those things! "I— I, uh."

"You said you would, man. Don't wanna be a liar, do ya?"

I sighed. "I suppose it's a small price I have to pay…to have my brother back."

"A friend loves at all times," a man's voice said from across the dark room. It was both mysterious and familiar.

We both looked into the dark part of the room, where someone was leaning against the wall. They walked forward into the light. "And a brother is born for adversity…an ancient Judaic proverb. It certainly rings true, does it not?"

"You," said Nick, his eyes narrowing. "What are you doing here?"

"You're the man who helped us down in the school's basement with the Shadow Mantis!" I said.

"I am," the man answered. Like last time, he was covered from head to toe with white and blue linen. His face was covered, like he was a ninja. The only thing visible were his eyes, which were dark but had a kind twinkle.

"Did *you* save Nick?" I asked.

He walked over to the bed and closed his eyes. He was quiet for a moment, then spoke. "Truly extraordinary things, Segols. As is the Edaniite that gives them their power."

"What does that have to do with—" I started to say.

"It was his own Edaniite that saved Nicklaus," the man said. "You see, when he took that rather nasty swim, the dark waters drained him of virtually all of his life energy. However, the Edaniite that supplies his Segol's power took over, giving his body an extra boost of energy."

Nick sat up straight. "So, I don't have any regular energy left, but the stuff that gives me my fire power is fueling my body right now?"

The man nodded.

"Well, I feel great!" he said, and his face did seem to have more color now.

The man crossed his arms. "You are very lucky, Nicklaus. If it were James or Abby, or possibly even Kelly, they would have died. You, however, have a larger reserve of Edaniite to fuel your rather combustive power. But even if your Edaniite reserves were half-full, you'd probably still be fighting for your life."

"Is that why you're here?" Nick asked. "To explain all this to us?"

"Not exactly," the man said. "I'm here to let you know that Abby and Kelly are in danger." He looked at me. "You've got to go help them, James."

"I'm going, too!" Nick exclaimed. He started to pull the electrodes off of his chest and stomach. One of them made a loud *pop* noise as he pulled it off, and left a circular, red mark on his belly. "Yowch!" he yelped.

"That is not wise," said the man. "Right now, your very life is tied to your Edaniite. If it runs out, you will die."

Nick held his index finger up, and a small, very bright red flame sparked up above it. "I got this. My team needs my help!" He blew the fire out.

"Nick," I said. "Maybe you should sit this one out… I mean, saved by Edaniite or not, you still have a temp of a hundred and seven. Biologically speaking, you should not even be coherent right now. Your brain should be frying."

"I'm going with ya, bro. That's all there is to it!" He started to get out of bed, but stopped. He laughed nervously. "Heh, heh, but maybe I shouldn't go when I'm half naked. Can't be all heroic in my boxer briefs!"

The strange man sighed and walked over to the dark corner of the room and grabbed a few things. He walked back and handed them to Nick. It was his clothes and shoes. "I had a feeling you'd be stubborn. So, I got your clothes. I won't say you can't go. Just be careful." He looked at me. "Don't worry about his temperature. I'd wager that his current temperature is normal for him since he acquired his fire power."

"I see," I said, feeling a little foolish that I didn't realize that earlier. "So, that's why he was showing classic signs of hypothermia even though his temperature was on the higher scale of normal."

"Huh? You lost me," Nick said while he slipped his pants on.

"If your body has an average temperature of 107, and your blood and organs have adapted to such a high temperature, if it dropped to 99, it would be just like a normal person's temperature going from 98 to 90," I explained.

"And that's...bad?" Nick said, standing up to put his shirt on.

"Ye—" I was interrupted by a loud voice coming from the hallway outside.

"Is *this* where they moved him to?" a woman's voice said from the other side of the door. It was Dr. Gabrielle's voice. She barged into the room and looked at Nick. She stared at him for a moment while he was putting his shirt on, and her face turned a deep red.

"Eep!" she screamed, and quickly put her hands to her eyes and turned around. "I-I-I'm so sorry...I didn't know you were awake, and g-eh-etting dressed."

Nick laughed. "You can turn around now. I'm fully clothed."

She slowly turned around and peeked out of her hand. When she saw it really was safe, she removed her hand from her face and eased up. "Ahem, anyway, welcome back, Nicklaus."

"Thanks, short stuff!" he teased.

She rolled her eyes and glanced over at the strange man. "You—"

The man nodded to her. "Hello, Gabrielle, how are you? It's been a while."

"It's Dr. Gabrielle now," she said.

The man had an amused twinkle in his eyes. "I apologize, Doctor."

"What are you doing here?" she asked him.

"I was sent," he answered. "They said it was urgent."

"The organization sent…you?" she asked with legitimate surprise.

He nodded. "Indeed. Now, we must get these boys out of here so they can help their teammates. They're in dire need of assistance."

"Do you think it wise to let Nicklaus go?" Dr. Gabrielle inquired. "He's just woken up."

"I'm right here, you know?" said Nick.

The man glanced at him. "Truly, it is unwise, but his mind is set…and they may need him."

"You think they need fire to fight water?" Dr. Gabrielle asked. "That sounds a little counterintuitive."

"Water evaporates when it rises to a high enough temperature," the man said calmly.

"Fine, but let's just hope the same thing doesn't happen to him…" said Dr. Gabrielle.

"Still right here," Nick said.

Dr. Gabrielle ignored him. She continued to look at the robed man like he was some kind of puzzle that needed solving. "How are we going to get them out of here? F.E.S.P.A. has this place surrounded."

"Leave that to me," he said.

"Okay, but I'm going to have to give a full report when I get back to headquarters," she said. It almost sounded like she was scolding him.

He blinked at her. "You act as though I'm going to blow them up."

She looked him square in the eye. "Well, your tactics are known to be a bit…unorthodox."

"Oh, they'll be fine," the man said. He turned to us. "Now, boys. I need you to close your eyes. We need to hurry, otherwise we'll miss our window."

Nick and I looked at each other. Nick had the same nervous expression I imagine I had.

"I promise, you won't get blown up…" the man said like it was an amusing concept.

After a moment or two, we closed our eyes.

"Hmm," the man said. "I suppose I need to give it a few more seconds. I need to wait for the perfect time."

"Perfect time for what?" I asked.

He was counting down. "Three, two, one…now!"

Panic rushed into my mind. "Wait. Perfect time for—" I felt a sudden rush of heat. Then, my feet and ankles felt cold and wet. "—what?"

There was no answer.

I opened my eyes, and Nick and I were not in the hospital room. We weren't even in the hospital. We were in what looked like a ballroom of some sort, but we were standing in about a foot of water. The two chandeliers on the blue-and-black checkered ceiling shook and flickered. The water below us rippled violently. I lost my balance and fell into the cold water.

Nick pulled me up. "You alright, man?"

I nodded. "Yes, but where are we?"

"Dunno, but I don't think it's Kansas."

I looked at him and frowned. "Do you really think this is a time for movie references?"

"It's always time for movie references," he answered. "I'm surprised you got that, though!"

"Everyone knows that movie," I answered. "At any rate, I think that strange man…he must have teleported us somewhere."

"Ya know, this place reminds me of the evil waterpark a little bit…" Nick said, looking around.

"It certainly has the same atmosphere, doesn't it?"

"Hopefully the girls are around here somewhere," he said. "Hey! Abbs! Kelly!" he called, but the only answer he got was his own echo.

There was a set of double doors on the other side of the room. I waded toward them. "Let's see if they're through here."

I tried to use my Scan ability to sense their presence. I had done it before, back when we were in the Trial Room when we first acquired our Segols. But I had no luck this time. Nick joined me at the door. I went to open it, but the doorknob started to twist by itself. I took a step back.

We heard screaming on the other side of the door.

"I'd recognize those screams from anywhere!" Nick said, his eyes wide.

I opened the door, but the room was empty. There was a loud *SLAM* as a trap door on the ground right in front of us sealed back up.

# CHAPTER 10: TOP OF THE TOWER—JAMES

"What the heck happened to this place?" Nick said, looking around at the disastrous room.

It felt like we were in an apocalyptic rendition of a fairytale world. We had just stepped out of what looked like a castle that had been ravaged by an army. The ground was cracked, and there were broken layers of rubber grass and yellow brick everywhere. The ground itself looked like it was made of stone, and it was cracked and uneven, except for where the trap door was.

"I can't get the door to open," I said as I stomped on the trap door. It was a frustrating feeling, just missing Kelly and Abby by mere seconds.

"What do you think triggered it?" Nick asked.

I thought for a moment, then turned toward the castle door. "The knob turned before I even touched it. Did one of them try to open the door?"

I turned both knobs, but nothing happened. Nick tried a few times, and still, nothing.

"I dunno, maybe it was a one-time deal?" Nick suggested.

"Perhaps…" I said, looking down at the sealed door. "I do hope they're alright. We need to join them as soon as possible. That strange man said that they were in danger."

"Alright," he said. "Let's start looking around."

We split up. I walked over to my end, where a pond was hewn into the ground. Though, now there wasn't much water in it; it had almost completely drained. The wall above it was made of stone, just like the pond. It bulged out in some areas, like the stone had cracked but was filled back in rapidly. There were also fragments of what looked like a boat in the pond. Pieces of it were scattered everywhere. A large piece of wood had the name *S.S. Waterdrop* written on it.

"Find anything, J-Man?" Nick yelled.

"Nothing of particular interest," I called back. "Just a boat that exploded."

We met in the center of the room, where the broken corpses of plastic trees bent and twisted around themselves. One tree looked relatively unharmed, though.

"Hell-el-eloooo," a high-pitched voice said. It sounded like a pre-recorded voice that was staticky and broken. "Can you please hel-elp meeeee?"

Stuck on the highest branch of the intact tree was an animatronic doll's head of that Princess Waterdrop character.

"I seeeeem to be stu-ck," it said.

"Yeesh," said Nick. "What a creepy-looking face!"

The doll's left eye twitched. "How da-da-dare you!" it yelled. "You remind me of that naughtyyyy gir-gir-girl who insulted me so. I am a princess, for goodnessss sake-ake-ake!"

"Princess of what?" Nick talked back to it. "Severed heads that get stuck in trees? Where's the rest of you?"

The head made a staticky humming sound as its jaw unhinged. "Oh, the rest of me-eeeee got zapped by the other naughty gi-irl. She wrecked my entiiiiire castle!"

Nick smirked. "Way to go, Ms. Kelly!"

"You are a veryyyy naughty-ty-ty boy!" the doll head said.

"What are you gonna do about it?" Nick heckled.

The doll's jaw went back in place, then it opened its mouth back up, and razor-sharp teeth popped out of its metal gumline.

"Nick?" I said. "Maybe you should stop teasing the evil doll head?"

He tapped the tree with his finger. "Oh, it's stuck in a tree. What could it possibly do?"

The doll head shook itself loose from the tree and landed on the ground. As it landed, its jaws slammed shut and made a sickening *snap*.

"It's snack-ack-ack time!" the doll head chimed as it started to bounce toward us like a ball. It lunged toward Nick and he caught it like a basketball.

The doll screeched. Nick twitched and threw it at me. To my surprise, I caught it.

The doll screeched again, and I threw it back at Nick. Nick tossed it back to me. I threw it as hard as I could toward the wall. Unfortunately, with my lack of athletic skills, it only went a few feet and landed on the soft fake grass.

I picked up a rock as it started bouncing toward us again. I slammed the rock down onto the doll's head and smashed it. Water gushed out from under the rock, which then popped like a water balloon, splashing water on the ground.

"Wow, J-Man, you pulverized it!" Nick cheered.

"I did, didn't I?" I said proudly. "Now where are we supposed to go?"

"Everywhere in here looks caved in," he said. "Let's try going back into the castle thing and find a way down to where the girls are."

I nodded, and we made our way back into the castle.

We waded through the foot or so of water in the castle ballroom. A set of stairs that led up to a balcony was on the far side of the room, but nowhere led downward.

"Looks like we can't go down," I said.

"Up it is," Nick answered.

We walked up the stairs, which were covered by purple carpet that had severe water damage. The style of this place reminded me of Hotel Barbaas.

Antique furniture that seemed beyond repair. Beautiful yet eerie decor. The overall feeling of being trapped.

The door along the balcony wall did not fit the rest of the room. It was cast-iron, like something out of an old factory. Nick grabbed the handle and pulled, and the door slowly screeched open. Just as we walked in, the door slammed shut behind us and quickly vanished behind a torrent of water that solidified and morphed into a wall of iron and steaming pipes.

"Guess we can't go back that way," Nick said. He looked ahead. "Why do I feel like I'm in some kind of Freddy Krueger nightmare?"

"Is he the one with the baseball mask?" I asked.

Nick rolled his eyes. "No, that's Jason…and it's a hockey mask. Freddy is the guy with the burned-up face and Christmas sweater. You know, the one with the claw hands?"

"The one that attacks on Halloween?" I asked.

Nick sighed. "That's Michael Myers."

"The guy who played Austin Powers? He's a serial killer?" I said, shocked.

Nick chuckled. "That's Mike Myers, different person. Are you doing this on purpose?"

"Y-yes, of course I am…" I lied.

"Well, either way. I don't want to run into any of those guys in this place."

It *was* creepy in here. There was a long, narrow, dark corridor that had low-hanging pipes and gears grinding on the wall. The sound of broken, rusty machinery pumping and whirling and popping echoed in the distance and beyond that was the sound of rushing water.

We walked ahead, careful not to touch the pipes, as they looked red-hot. It was pretty cramped; the thinnest part of the corridor could only fit one of us at a time. My arm accidently touched one of the hot pipes.

"Ouch!" I cried as searing pain burned into my arm.

"You okay?" Nick asked, walking behind me.

I grabbed my arm. "Yes, it's just these pipes are really hot."

"What're you touching them for?" he asked.

"I didn't mean to!"

Finally, we reached the end of the narrow path, which opened into a wide, open space. A spiral staircase wound up into the darkness of the impossibly high ceiling.

"Better start climbin'," Nick said.

"Must we?" I answered, looking up. It looked like way too much physical activity.

Nick started to jog up the stairs.

I heard one of the pipes behind me hiss threateningly, and then I thought about what Nick said about Mike Myers, or was it Jason? At any rate, it gave me a fright, as irrational as it was. "Wait for me!" I yelled up at him.

"Hurry it up," Nick answered. He was already halfway up the stairs.

"You really shouldn't be running like that, anyway. You were in a coma twenty minutes ago!"

"Naah, I feel great!" he yelled back.

*He can be so irresponsible!* I thought to myself.

Nick reached the top of the stairs roughly forty-five seconds before I did. I stumbled up after him, huffing and puffing.

I tried to speak. "Wait—*huff*—for me—*wheeze*—"

"We gotta work on your stamina, J-Man," Nick said, crossing his arms.

"I'm fine—*huff*— I just feel like dying a little."

"C'mon, we gotta get moving," Nick said. When he turned around to go through the tall archway at the top of the stairs, he fell over and grabbed the handrail for balance.

"Are you okay?" I asked, offering to help him back up.

He refused help and got back to his feet. He smiled. "Guess I overexerted myself a little bit there." For a brief moment, his face was pale and tired.

"You need to be careful," I said worriedly. "Remember, you're only working off of your Edaniite right now. You have no life energy to spare."

"Alright, Mom, I'll take it easy," he said as he let go of the handrail.

We walked through the archway and wound up in a semi-circle hallway. We walked around the bowed structure and found another door at the end of the room.

It was a small door, about five feet high. It had cushy yellow fabric with red buttons that formed a square in the middle, and a purple, crystal doorknob. It looked just as out of place as the iron door in the waterlogged castle. In fact, this door and that one would have been perfect if they switched places with each other.

I turned the knob and opened the door, and we both had to duck down to enter the room.

We walked into what looked like a giant, circular playroom. It had a black-and-purple checkered ceiling, with six light fixtures that looked like a toddler had made them hanging from it. The lights were made from black and purple blocks, and were so asymmetrical they made my head hurt.

The floor was also checkered tile, alternating black and purple. In the center of the room was a giant dollhouse, about seven feet high. It was a miniature model of the castle, but the double doors were almost as tall as the castle itself.

The lights above us suddenly brightened, and eerie carnival music started to play. The voice of Princess Waterdrop suddenly filled the room. "Welcome, welcome, to my playroom! I'm sure you'll enjoy the pint-sized parade of the charismatic characters of Wacky Water World!"

The doors of the castle creaked open, and a three-foot tall plushy doll of Princess Waterdrop walked out. It was just as creepy as the animatronic doll head. This doll's eyes were made of pitch-black buttons, and its mouth was stitched into a permanent, black grin.

"Okay, this is creeping me out," said Nick, wrinkling his nose.

"The doll is a little unnerving," I said. "Wait, did it say something about a parade?" That made me feel uneasy.

The plushy doll reached for its back and pulled a string. "Hello, are you ready to play?" it asked in a slow, polite voice, but its mouth didn't move. "I'm having a party. A parade partyyyy," Its voice slowed and lowered to a baritone at the word *party*. It pulled on its string again, and its voice was high-pitched once more. "Ahem, now, let's invite the rest of our guests, shall we?"

The doll raised its hands, and its body began to rotate. The lower half of its body rotated clockwise, while its top half rotated counterclockwise.

Small openings appeared in each of the walls, and dozens of plushy and porcelain dolls started to crawl out of them. There were at least six different renditions of Princess Waterdrop, including one with a broken neck and a crack on its head just above its right eye. There were four or five different Wacky Williams and three water-dragon plushies that slithered out of the walls. Creepy porcelain dolls of winged children with little bows and arrows flew clumsily out of some of the openings, as did several green-hued witch dolls on broomsticks. All of the anthropomorphic dolls gathered around us.

"We're surrounded by a bunch of deformed toys..." Nick muttered. "They're so creepy, I kinda wish I was back in that coma," he joked, but I did not find it amusing.

The plushy doll that stood in the castle doorway stopped rotating and faced us. It pulled on its cord again. "That can be arranged, dear. Here at Wacky Water Tower, dreams can come true. Now, let's play!"

The army of dolls began to rush us. All of the Princess Waterdrop dolls had razor-sharp teeth that poked out of their mouths. The Wacky Williams were all juggling tiny little explosives. The dragons shot out scalding-hot water. The winged children shot sharp little arrows, and the witches blew black, putrid-smelling gas out of the end of their brooms.

Nick and I tried stepping on them, but they got back up and kept attacking.

"This is ridiculous!" Nick yelled. "I'm gonna torch 'em!"

"No!" I said before he made a fireball.

"Why not?" he asked impatiently.

"You don't want to waste your power. Remember the thing where you can die if you run out of Edaniite? Only use your power as a last resort!"

Two Wacky William dolls and the broken Princess Waterdrop lunged toward him. He kicked them as hard as he could, and they all flew toward the castle, shattered, and turned into puddles of water. The larger Princess Waterdrop plushy, still standing at the castle doors, pulled its cord again. "You won't beat us that easily," it said. Its black stitched mouth ripped open, revealing its razorblade teeth. It let out a terrible screech. The puddles of water rose from the floor and re-formed into dolls.

A witch and a child both flew at me. I grabbed them both and slammed them into each other, and they shattered and liquified. The Waterdrop doll screeched again, and they were restored, too. When it screeched again after Nick destroyed a witch doll, which promptly reformed, I noticed a pattern.

"Nick, we need to destroy that doll!" I pointed at the screaming princess. "It's repairing the ones that we break."

Nick was stomping and kicking at the other dolls. "Gladly!" he yelled back. He kicked several of the dolls at the screamer.

They all hit the doll and liquified, but the screeching doll rose out of the puddle of water and bared its razor-sharp teeth at us. It began to float in the air. Suddenly, it lunged toward Nick and started screeching again, and all of the broken dolls re-formed behind it.

The screeching doll opened its mouth wide and implanted itself into Nick's right shoulder. He yelled out in a mix of pain and annoyance. "G-get off of me, Anabelle!" he yelled as he tried pulling it off of him.

Before I could help him, I was tripped by a water dragon brigade. They expelled hot water on me. The winged children aimed and shot me in the leg with a bunch of arrows, each feeling like a bee sting.

I looked up at Nick. He was stumbling around, trying to pull the doll out of his shoulder. "I…am…not…about…to…lose…to…a…bunch…of…stupid…toys!" He managed to pull the doll off of him. It spat a ripped, bloody part of his shirt in his face. It pulled the cord on its back and laughed at him. He suddenly chucked it across the room as hard as he could, and it flew at breakneck speed at the wall, laughing as it flew through the air.

Above me, a legion of witch dolls were dive-bombing me. The cackling Princess Waterdrop doll hit the wall with a shatter, followed by a splash. The diving witch dolls turned into water and splashed me in the face. All of the other dolls began to liquify and come apart, creating a thin layer of water all over the floor.

Nick grabbed his hurt shoulder and rotated it. "I hope that thing didn't have some kind of disease. And look what it did to my shirt!" His shoulder was visible and bleeding. He walked over to me and helped me up. "Bro, what happened to your face?" he asked. "It looks like it got sunburned or something."

"The dragons scalded me with water," I said. I tried to walk, but a sharp pain shot up my leg. I limped to the wall closest to me. "And the flying children shot me with their arrows."

Nick laughed. "We just got beat up by a bunch of toys! Good thing Abbs and Kelly didn't see this!"

I grinned. "Quite embarrassing, indeed."

"Let's tell 'em we fought off an entire army of monsters," he said. "Sounds more heroic."

"Just leave out the part about them being tiny?" I said.

"Yeah, do you want them to make fun of us? They wouldn't let us live it down for months!"

"They would not have been able to handle it much better."

Nick chuckled, but grabbed his still-bleeding shoulder. "True that. I can just imagine how freaked Abbs would be with the clown dolls!"

"Jesters, technically."

"Yeah, yeah, yeah. Anyway, now where are we headed?"

There was a staircase behind the castle dollhouse that I did not notice before. "I suppose we go up," I said, nodding toward it.

The stairs led to a door on the ceiling, which led outside. We stepped out onto the roof of…wherever we were. It was a large, flat, circular roof with no rails or guards around it. Nick walked over to the edge and looked down.

He whistled. "That sure is a looong way down," he said.

I shuffled my way next to him and glanced over the edge. He was not kidding. It looked like a two-hundred-foot fall at least! I gasped and took a giant step backward. "I would very much like to go back downstairs."

"What's wrong, J-Man? Scared of heights?"

I slowly nodded. "I am, as a matter of fact. The Illusion Tree was bad enough. I had to gather all of my rather meager supply of courage to jump off of *it*. But we are much higher up now."

Nick backed away from the edge. "Yeah, I guess it is kind of a drop down."

The floor below us began to rumble, and I ran to the center of the roof.

There was a booming, low-pitched growl.

"Bro, was that you? You hungry or somethin'?" Nick asked.

"That was not me," I answered. I pointed behind me. "It came from—"

Nick's eyes widened.

I slowly turned around to see what he was gawking at.

A gargantuan serpentine, animatronic creature rose from the other side of the building and started circling the air above us like a vulture. It was at least sixty feet long. Its metallic blue-green scales glimmered in the pale-yellow sunlight. It looked down at us with its burning red eyes and let out a predatory screech.

It started its dive. Nick and I looked at each other, then ran for it. The sound of the giant monster's metallic frame was getting closer and closer. We ran back toward the stairs, but the door was gone!

"Dive!" Nick yelled.

We lunged to the ground and crashed. My leg was pulsing with pain. The dragon swooped down and almost got us, missing by a mere foot. It circled the roof and flew at us again. It opened its large mouth, and scalding hot water sprayed out of it like a geyser.

I rolled out of the way, but Nick got doused.

"Nick!" I yelled as the boiling water crashed down on him.

I ran toward him, and large drops of the water splashed all over my body. It was much hotter than the dragon doll's water. This felt like it could boil the flesh off of you if you were in it for more than two minutes.

The scalding waterfall diminished, and Nick was still standing, although he was breathing a little heavily. But his skin did not look red at all.

He chuckled at the dragon, who was circling around the roof, ascending as it did.

"I've had ice baths that felt hotter than that!" he chided.

I looked at my own skin; the parts where the water had touched were as red as a rose. *But, how is he not burned? Oh, yes!* I thought. *Because of his body's natural temperature from his fire abilities.*

The dragon began to dive again, this time much faster.

"J-Man?" Nick said. "Would this be considered an emergency situation?"

"What do you mean?" I answered.

"Would this be a good time to blow things up?"

"Ah, yes…I would say that this is the perfect time. Just don't overdo it!"

"Psh, do I ever?" he asked in a cheerful tone. I assumed that was a rhetorical question.

The dragon was mere feet from us.

"This is gonna be fun!" Nick yelled as he leaped as high as he could and landed on the dragon's neck.

The robotic serpent let out an enraged cry and began whipping and thrashing in the air. A fireball surrounded Nick's fist and he punched the nape of the dragon's neck. The dragon's head burst like a giant water balloon, and the rest of its body popped open in segments. Water began to fall in a large cascade and swept me up as Nick fell, tucked, and rolled.

The water was hot, but not scalding. It sent me toward the edge of the roof. I let out a yell as the water spilled over the roof. I grabbed on to the slickening edge. It was hard to hold on.

"I gotcha!" Nick yelled as he grabbed my arm and pulled me up.

Once I caught my balance, Nick grabbed his shoulder. He had used his injured arm to pull me up. He was breathing even heavier, and his face was paler than before.

He looked at me and smiled. "You're—*huff*—a lot heavier than—*huff*—you look!"

"Why'd you grab me with your bad arm?" I asked.

He shrugged. "Didn't really have time to think."

"Are you okay?" I asked. "You look a little rough. Is it because of your shoulder or is it because you used your Segol?"

"I'm fine," he insisted between breaths. "But how're we gonna get down?"

I glanced downward, and my vision blurred. I quickly looked away. "I don't know, but we need to think of something, and fast. I really do not like it up here."

Nick looked down for a moment. He pointed to the left. "How about that?"

I looked in the direction he was pointing. Two large, white stone platforms were moving on their own. One was going up and down, the other left and right.

Nick walked toward the platform. I followed him.

"That looks like at least a ten-foot plunge, if we're lucky. If we are not, then it looks like a two-hundred-foot drop," I said, feeling a little nauseous.

Nick looked at the platform for a moment. "Sorry, man."

"For wha—" He linked his arm with mine and jumped off the roof. "Aaaah!" I yelled as we fell and landed on the platform.

"For that," he said, grinning at me.

My lungs were fighting for oxygen. "Are you trying to kill me?" I said, exasperated.

Nick's face got serious. "No, why would I try to kill you? We're brothers, remember?"

I grabbed my chest. "So were Cain and Abel!"

The platform was moving slowly downward.

"Alright, now we gotta jump to the next one," he said, looking down at it. "I think I see a window or something down there."

"Meaning…we have to jump again?" I asked. I really didn't want to.

He smiled obnoxiously. "You don't wanna to stay up here for the rest of your life, do ya?"

He did have a point. "Alright, if we must," I relented.

"We'll be fine, we just need to time it right is all."

I held my breath.

"Ready, J-Man?"

I nodded.

"Alright…now!" he yelled as he jumped to the other platform.

I jumped after him. I barely made it to the platform and almost fell off.

"Our future assignments better be on ground level at all times!" I said, trying to catch my breath.

The platform started to move slowly to the right, toward a large window. About halfway there, Nick turned to look at something.

"No way!" he exclaimed.

"Don't yell like that up here!" I said breathlessly.

"Look!" He pointed at something stuck in the wall.

It was a small, flat round object. Half of it was sticking out, and in its center was a sapphire.

"Is that…the Ark?" I said, in disbelief.

Nick grabbed it when the we got close enough. He tried to pull it out, but it didn't budge. He pulled harder, but it barely moved. He yanked on it as hard as he could, and it shot out of the wall. He toppled over and almost fell off of the platform.

"Got it!" Nick said, standing back up, grinning proudly.

"Yes, but you almost fell and died," I said. This whole mission was going to give me an ulcer. Or a heart attack. Or both.

"Nah, I wasn't even close to falling!" Nick said.

We reached the large window. Nick slammed the Ark against the window, and the shattered glass melted into droplets of water. We hopped into an ordinary-looking room with a large pool.

There was a door on the other side of the room. As we walked toward it, Nick looked at the Ark and frowned. "If this is the real Ark, and this place was made by the villains, how come it didn't melt the building or blow it up, like with the big bug?"

I thought for a moment. "It could be because the barrier has been shattered. I think the barrier is what contains the Edaniite, not the Ark itself. Or, it could be that the Ark does contain minute traces of Edaniite on its own, but it is such a scant amount that it doesn't cause injury to the

Corrupted."

"Sure, we'll go with that," said Nick, half paying attention.

We reached the door and walked through it. We were in the middle of a very long set of stairs.

"More stairs," said Nick.

"Better than floating platforms…" I muttered.

We started to walk down. About halfway, the steps folded, turning the staircase into a long, winding slide. We rode it down and skidded across the floor. The staircase suddenly slid into the walls and vanished from sight.

"This place looks familiar," I said as I stood up and observed our surroundings. "It looks like…a mirrored image of Wacky Water World's indoor park lobby."

Nick raised an eyebrow. "Yeah, if you're lookin' through a funhouse mirror, maybe."

We heard screams coming from behind us.

I turned around. "It's coming from the theater!"

We ran toward the theater and up the stairs, and my leg started hurting again.

We entered the theater and tried going into the auditorium, but it was gated off. We ran up the staircase to try the doors on the second floor, but the doors weren't even there!

Nick ran back downstairs and started to stretch. "I'll take care of this."

"You aren't going to blow the gate up, are you?" I asked as I hobbled behind him.

"Don't need to," he said. He sprinted and kicked part of the gate down. He stumbled and fell over to the other side of it. He got up. "See? Piece of cake!"

I stepped over the opening he made.

More screams came from somewhere above. We looked up and saw someone falling from the catwalk. It was too dark to see who it was, and they were falling too fast for us to catch them. They crashed right in front of us with a loud *splash!*

It was a Wacky William animatronic! It was facing upward. The back of its head, as well as its right arm and most of its left leg, had been liquified into clear water. Its face was seeping droplets of water as it gargled a broken-up laugh.

Nick looked up, then back down at the liquifying jester. "Guess we all *don't* float down here, after all," he said, and started howling with laughter. I did not get the joke.

# CHAPTER 11: TORN TOWER—ABBY

The animatronic freak leaped at us, its cackle filling the air. Kelly held her hands out in front of her, and they started to glow. Purple light surrounded Wacky William, and the life-sized doll was suspended in the air, just inches away from us. Kelly swung both hands to the left, and William was thrown over the catwalk. A few seconds later, there was a loud *splash* from below.

Kelly carefully sat down on the catwalk and let out a breath of relief.

I smiled at her. "Kelly, you are totally my hero. Thank goodness we don't have to worry about that stupid clown anymore."

As soon as I said that, a burst of laughter echoed up from the theater.

Kelly cringed. "Is that the clown?"

"No," I said, listening carefully to the laughter. *Am I hearing things? I* thought. *It couldn't be... That sounds like...* I looked over the edge of the catwalk to see if it was true.

"Hey, Abbs!" Nick yelled up, waving at me. It was him! James was there, too.

Kelly stood up so quickly she almost stumbled off the catwalk as she looked over the edge. "You're alive!" she yelled with a wide smile on her face.

"You're not gonna get rid of me that easily!" he called.

"Hold on!" I yelled. "We'll be down there in a minute!"

Kelly and I crept our way back down the catwalk and sprinted down the stairs.

We ran through the theater and reunited with the boys. Kelly hugged Nick and almost knocked him over. She buried her face in his chest. "I thought you were gone…" she whispered.

Nick struggled as she squeezed the air out of him. "*Cough*— You didn't really think a little water was gonna keep me down, did you?"

She let go of him and backed away, looking down at herself. "Why…are you soaked?" She gently touched his shoulder. "And you're hurt!"

"Yeah, well, we had a few close calls," he said with a shrug.

"We did, too," I said, showing him my arm.

Kelly showed him her leg.

"Are you guys okay?" he asked, looking at us with concern.

"Yeah, you should see the other guys," Kelly said.

"I think we did," said James. "The Princess Waterdrop doll. The wrecked room outside of the castle." He pointed at the slowly dissolving Wacky William on the floor. "Him."

Kelly cringed. "Ugh. I can't decide which was worse, the princess or the clown." My vote was the clown, but the princess was a very close second.

"The Princess Waterdrop animatronic was pretty disturbing…" James said.

"Yeah," Nick said, wrinkling his nose. "The thing had a buzzsaw that popped out of its mouth!"

"It was still alive?" I asked as my whole body tightened.

"Only its head," Nick said. "But J-Man took care of that." He chuckled. "Crushed that thing flat with a rock like a savage!"

"I would blush," James said with a coy smile. "But my face is already red…"

"Why *is* your face so red?" I asked.

He and Nick looked at each other, then he looked back at me. "Three mechanical water dragons poured searing water onto me. We had to fight off a whole horde of animatronic monsters. I also got shot in the leg by several arrows," said James, pointing to his leg. His jeans had at least a dozen punctures with some stains of red.

"How do you still have a leg if you got shot by a bunch of arrows?" Kelly asked.

James almost looked embarrassed. "I…well, the arrows were pretty small."

Nick snickered.

"What's so funny?" Kelly asked. "He got attacked. I don't get the joke."

"Nothing," Nick said, trying not to laugh. "You wouldn't get it. You, uh, had to be there. It's a *little* inside joke." He winked at James.

The whole place started to rumble.

"Why does this place keep shaking?" Nick yelled, holding on to one of the theater seats.

"I don't know, but let's try to get out of here," I said. "Marina said that if we get to the top of the tower within the time limit, we'll get out of this freaky place and back to the real world. And I think we have just enough time to—"

"She was lying," James said. "We were up there, and all we saw was a large robotic dragon."

"Are you kidding me?" I said as both anger and fear filled my stomach. I couldn't say I was surprised, though. I mean, why would that witch let us escape when we were in her grasp?

"That wouldn't be much of a joke, Abbs," Nick said. He paused, and snapped his finger. "Oh, yeah!" he yelled, and pulled something out of his pocket. "We found this up there!" He handed it to me.

I looked down, and I felt a jolt of excitement. "It's the—"

"Yup," Nick said. "Me and J-Man found it stuck in the wall."

The Ark's sapphire gemstone brightened, and I suddenly felt warm and energized.

I hugged Nick so hard he almost fell over the seat.

"Now we just need to find a way out of here," said Kelly.

We ran to the entrance of the auditorium. The gate that blocked it off was broken. I didn't even have to ask what happened. My brother's a pretty good demolitionist.

"Ladies first," Nick said.

Kelly started to walk toward it, but was blasted back by a powerful geyser that quickly solidified into a wall. Long, narrow spikes shot out of it and almost impaled her.

She rolled back and quickly got to her feet.

A splashing sound came from the entrance to the catwalk, and a pillar of water shot out in front of that door and solidified into part of the wall.

"Now what're we supposed to do?" I asked. "How're we going to get out of here?"

"Perhaps there is an exit behind the stage," James suggested.

"It was pitch black when we were back there, so it's possible we missed one," said Kelly.

"I'll go back there as long as another Wacky William doll doesn't pop up out of nowhere," I said with a shiver.

"Looks like you guys took care of the last one," Nick said, looking down at the puddle that was Wacky William.

"We don't want an encore, believe me," I said.

We went to the stage and climbed the steps. Before we could get backstage, water began to drip out of the batten that held up the curtains. The drops of water became heavier and heavier, and eventually became a waterfall that concealed the entire backstage. The waterfall formed itself into a giant portrait of Princess Waterdrop and Wacky William. It was absolutely hideous. They were both horribly cross-eyed and smiled sadistically, and each of them had deformed, crooked blackened teeth.

We backed away from the newly formed wall. Precisely at center stage, another pillar of water shot up from the floor to the ceiling. As the water crashed against the ceiling, it flowed outward and covered the entire theater's ceiling. As it reached the edges, the water trickled down each wall in streams that branched out like blood vessels. The central pillar of water expanded, sending scalding-hot water everywhere, rushing the four of us offstage.

We struggled to get up as the water pushed us against the theater seats. When the water finally subsided, we had to use the now-soaked theater seats for support.

Marina stood center stage, and she looked like a hot mess. It looked like her hair lost a fight with a kitchen beater. Her kimono was tattered, and her rage-filled eyes seemed to glow a subtle reddish-color. Her nails were long and sharp. Her breathing was harsh and angry.

She glared at Nick. "I have two questions for you, boy," she said in an angry, raspy tone. "First, how are you still alive? You were drained of all of your life energy!"

"Tch, I'm not gonna tell you, sea hag!" He paused for a moment. "But it's mostly because I'm not exactly sure how to explain it."

"Very well, then," she hissed. "Please, answer my second question. How did you get into my tower? Nobody has ever infiltrated my dimension before!"

"Not exactly sure of that, either," he said with perfect honesty in his voice. "You'd have to ask the ninja dude."

"Ninja dude?" Kelly repeated.

James nodded. "Yes, the gentleman that helped us in the basement when we faced the Shadow Mantis. He got us here somehow."

"Well," Marina said in a calmer voice as her hair straightened, her eyes became its normal azure color, and her nails retracted to normal size. "Trespassing is quite rude!" she said in her dignified, obnoxiously ladylike tone.

"You want to talk rude?" I yelled back up at her. "You lied about us getting out of here if we got to the top of the tower!"

"Just a well-mannered jest," she said, slipping her hands in opposite sleeves. "The rude ones are the four of you. I was merely returning the favor. You killed my sister and now I'll kill you." She giggled. "I will rather enjoy drowning you in sorrow."

"That plant freak was your sister?" I retorted.

Marina glowered at me with a paralyzing gaze. She held her arms out, and they turned into large streams of water that rushed toward me. Giant liquid hands rushed out of the streams and grabbed me, and I was dragged onstage. When I reached Marina, her hands and arms returned to normal. She gripped me tightly by my shirt. For such a dainty-looking girl, she sure had a strong grip. I couldn't free myself.

She lifted me up. "That is my sister you're talking about, you wretched girl." She glanced at my hand, I was still holding the Ark. She grinned at me. "But I suppose I can forgive you since you did deliver the Ark to me."

"In your dreams!" I said, and spat in her face.

"You vile little—" She looked at my arm and smiled. "Oh, my dear little urchin, you seem to have hurt your arm. Let me clean it out for you."

Water trickled from Marina's hand and onto my arm. It slithered up my arm and into my cut. Seething pain surged through my wound as the water seeped into my skin. Marina giggled at my screams of agony.

"My, my, my. What a beautiful singing voice you have," she said gleefully.

Pain started to spread throughout my whole arm. It felt like it was being skewered by a million tiny, icy knives. As my arm spasmed in pain, I dropped the Ark.

Marina's giggling stopped. Her body started to bubble like she had a plague of boils. In an instant, she exploded, and I fell to my knees. I looked over on stage right and saw the others. Nick had his hands held out.

I grabbed the Ark, got to my feet and stumbled over to them. I held on to my aching arm, it felt like it was going to fall off.

Nick was trembling and almost toppled over, but managed to catch himself by leaning against the stair rail. His face was pale, and his breathing was labored. "Are…you…okay?" he asked me.

"I could ask the same thing," I said, groaning a little in pain. "What's wrong with you?"

James looked at Nick with deep concern. "Marina was correct… He *did* lose all of his life energy. However, his Edaniite is supplying him with its own power to keep him alive. Using his ability diminishes his supply of Edaniite. If he uses enough of it…he could still die."

"*What?*" Kelly squeaked as she looked at him with deep concern.

Nick looked at her and smiled, but it was an exhausted, ghastly smile. "I'm fine, don't worry."

A waterspout shot up center stage, and Marina reformed out of it. "Tsk, tsk, tsk. You'll never defeat me that way." She slowly strutted toward us.

Kelly's hand started to glow with golden light. "Oh, I have *so* been looking forward to doing this!" She threw a bolt of lightning straight toward Marina.

Marina gasped. "Oh, dear!" she said as the bolt got closer. The stream of electricity divided in two right before it hit her, circled around her, and reconnected behind her. It zoomed across the stage and hit the wall on the far side. The bolt of electricity boomed and shot up the wall, creating a jagged line up to the ceiling. The entire room shook from the blast. The wall quickly repaired itself as a stream of water moved up the wall.

Kelly backed up. "H-how did you?"

Marina giggled. "I can't be touched by your lightning for the same reason

I can't be frozen in time. Must be a terrible disappointment for you. Most of your attacks can't even touch me, and the one that *is* strong enough to cross the divide cannot destroy me." She bared her nails, which sharpened into talons. "Now, who would like to die first?"

She looked at James and grinned wickedly. "How about you, little boy? I mean, it's not like you contribute much to the group, anyway." She lunged toward him.

Nick shot both of his hands up toward Marina and let out a painful groan. She exploded in midair.

"Let's…move it," Nick said weakly, barely able to stand.

The three of us helped Nick catch his balance, and we moved across the stage.

*There has to be a way to beat her,* I thought. *There just has to be… I can't freeze her. Kelly can't zap her. What can we do? The only thing that works on her is Nick's power, but she just— Wait, that's it!*

Nick stopped walking and stooped over. He grabbed his chest and started coughing violently, his face whiter than a ghost's.

Kelly patted his back. "Nick…you're overdoing it."

He caught his breath and stood up straight. "I'm…okay, just breathed in…some spit is all."

"Don't think I believe *that* for one second, Nicklaus!" she scolded.

"Guys, I think I know how to beat this hag!" I said.

They all looked at me.

"Kelly, can you make another thunderbolt?" I asked her.

She held out her hand, and it started to glow with golden light. "Yes…but probably only one more."

A water spout shot up from the other side of the stage and formed back into Marina. "I really wish you would stop doing that." She started to walk in our direction, nails bared.

I turned to my brother. I really didn't want to ask this of him, but we didn't have much choice. "Can you manage to blow her up one more time?"

Kelly put her foot down. "Are you crazy? Look at him. He's about to keel over!"

James looked perplexed. "Why would you…" He looked at Marina, who was standing in the center of the stage, then at Kelly's glowing hand. His eyes brightened. "Ah, I understand. Abby, you are a genius! But…I do not think Nick can—"

"Of course I can," Nick said, trying to sound tough, but his voice was weak and cracking.

Kelly placed her nonelectrified hand on his shoulder. "Nick…"

"Let me do this, Kelly," he said, gently but insistent.

Marina's nails elongated even more. Her hair began to hover above her head. "I hope you're ready now, dears."

Nick took a deep breath. His hands and legs were shaking. He lifted his hands and aimed them at Marina. He flicked both hands like he was throwing something.

Marina's body started to bubble, but not as much as before. She took a long, labored step forward. "Doesn't pack much of a punch now, cutie. You don't look so well. Perhaps you need a calming dip to settle your nerves!"

Nick held his hands up toward Marina. His whole body was trembling from the strain. A stream of blood ran from his nose. He thrust his hands forward again, and Marina burst apart, creating a puddle of water on the floor.

Nick stumbled like a drunk, but caught himself. He winced with every breath.

"Kelly, throw the lightning bolt where she was standing," I said, trying to focus on the task at hand. I really hated myself for making my brother use his Segol again when clearly he was running out of the very power that was keeping him alive.

Kelly looked at Nick, her face haunted with worry.

"Go on…Kelly," Nick said raspily.

She took a deep breath and threw a bolt of lightning toward center stage.

I flicked my hands toward the bolt, and it froze in place.

The puddle of water sprang up, and Marina reappeared, but the stream of electricity was frozen in place right in her stomach.

She looked annoyed. "You foolish children. I am about to drown every one of you in the worst way possible."

"You may want to look down, hag," I said, pointing at her stomach. "I think you're going to be shocked at what you see."

She looked down. "Wh-what's this?" she said in a panicked voice.

I waved at her. "Buh-bye."

Her face twisted in fear. "Wait—" she said as she tried to move. The stream of electricity unfroze inside of her. The intense electrical current ran through her body and she started glowing like a Christmas tree. She let out a loud scream and burst open. Water sprayed everywhere.

There was a long silence, and she didn't reform.

"We did it!" I said, feeling so gratified I thought I would burst open too.

"Finally," said James, relaxed.

Nick smiled. "Good job, guys…now let's get out of here so we can get some rest—" He started to cough violently, then started gasping for breath.

I took a step toward him. "Nick?"

His whole body tremored, and his eyes rolled to the back of his head. He collapsed and Kelly caught him, but she fell over too.

The theater started to shake more violently than before as drops of water began to fall from above. The ground felt soft and wet. The theater seats began to lose their form and liquify.

"This is not good," said James as he looked around frantically. "With Marina gone so abruptly, this place is going to fall apart."

The walls started to rip and tear, with large cracks running up and down them like they had been sliced open by some giant, invisible monster.

The floor suddenly liquified completely, and we fell into the water. I was sucked under. The frigid water roared in my ears as I struggled to kick up to the surface.

I emerged out of the water. "Is everyone okay?" I called.

James popped his head up a few feet away. "I am."

"We're here!" Kelly yelled. She was six or seven feet away, struggling to keep an unconscious Nick above water. She held him up with intense determination, but she could hardly stay afloat herself.

James and I started to swim toward them. The loud roaring became unbearable as the cracks in the wall started to become large gashes. I could hear the muffled screams of people coming from the other side. Water began to leach out of the tears in the wall into the other side. After a moment, the water started to pour back in, and people were dragged into the room. They were all trying to stay afloat, grabbing whatever they could. But everything they grabbed on to would simply liquify and melt into the swelling water.

The water began to pour back out. James and I fell out of this room and into another. It was Wacky William's theater in the real world.

"We need to get back to the other side and help Nick and Kelly!" James yelled.

I nodded. More people poured out of the gashes in the wall like schools of doomed fish, and the water rushed out of the other side like geysers. We were being forced away from the wall, away from Nick and Kelly.

Then, like we were on some kind of topsy-turvy board, the water reversed direction, and we started moving back toward the Water Tower dimension. James and I were thrown in by the rapid water, along with dozens of other people. I looked around the quickly dissolving room, but I couldn't see Kelly or Nick. Then I lost James too!

"Guys!" I screamed. I couldn't hear them over the frantic cries of the other people trapped in the water.

There was a loud creaking sound. I looked up at the broken wall that separated the tower's theater from Wacky Water World's. It rippled and shook before it completely liquified and became a tidal wave. The giant wall of water crashed down on top of everyone. A second later, everything that was left of the tower theater dissolved into water.

Now we were in Wacky Water World's theater, and more people were being thrown into the rapidly increasing flow. The water reached the second-story balcony. People were trying to escape, but the water spilled over the balcony and swept them into its cruel, icy grasp.

There was another loud rumble, and everything in the theater started to liquify, too! The wall that separated it from the rest of the Wacky Water World building vanished with a roaring splash, and everyone in the theater spilled out into the lobby. Water quickly filled the entire indoor structure of the park. So many people were splashing around helplessly around me, I could hardly stay afloat. I felt slaps and kicks of desperate people trying to stay above water. In the far corner of the room, the water coaster was dissolving into the flood. Those aboard were dragged into the currents below.

*This is awful*, my mind screamed. *Did we do this? Did…I do this? This was my idea, after all. Because we roasted Marina, are all of these people going to drown?*

The place rumbled violently, and the entire building around us collapsed under the water. Parts of the ceiling fell on people, but right before the chunks of ceiling struck them, they became large bursts of water. The walls liquified, and the entire body of water spilled outside. We were basically on top of a fifty-foot wave as it crashed onto the ground below. The wave swept everything and everyone in its wake. Every structure within the confines of the park became water, adding to the volume of the wave. Finally, after the water had consumed and melded with everything else in the park, it gushed out into the abandoned parking lot and into the woods behind it.

People landed on top of cars; some were swept under them. A few people were dragged into the woods and thrown down the cliffs that overlooked the vast ocean of trees below.

The roar of the water muddled the people's terrified cries as I was thrown forward. I crashed into a mound of dirt just outside of the parking lot. I struggled to stand to my feet, my balance was wobbly, but I managed. James face-planted into the dirt mound that was now more like a giant swamp of mud. I helped him up, and he had that "I need to bleach myself to kill all of the germs" look on his face. His glasses were gone, and he spat mud out of his mouth. "Wh-where are the others?" he yelled.

My eyes darted to and fro, and I spotted them about thirty feet away. "I see them!" I cried. I grabbed him by the hand and moved as fast as I could toward them.

Kelly was on top of the Tunnel of Love sign that was quickly disintegrating into water. Nick was lying face-up on top of her. He was still unconscious. His whole body was glowing a faint purple. Taking a closer look, I saw that he was hovering a few inches above Kelly.

She was panting, struggling for breath. Her hands were at her sides, her palms faced upward and flickering with purple light. She was so exhausted, she didn't even acknowledge our presence. The purple light around her hands and Nick's body went out, and she fainted as Nick fell on top of her.

James wiped the mud from his eyes. "Are they…alive?"

I knelt down to them for a closer look. They were both breathing. "Yes, but—"

"But what?" he said in a panic. "I can't see."

"Kelly. She…she kept him above water by using her gravity power this whole time."

James gasped. "That must have put a great strain on her body. How did she stay afloat?"

"She managed to find a ride sign to float on that didn't dissolve 'til just now."

"Ride sign? Which one?"

I smiled at the cute irony of it. "It doesn't matter. What matters is that they're safe."

James squinted, and looked around us. "What about everyone else? I wonder how many people were caught up in the water. I hope everyone made it out okay."

"Me, too," I said, but I doubted that everyone had gotten out of there with their lives.

# CHAPTER 12: RAINY DAYS—ABBY

According to Edania Organization intelligence, the incident at Wacky Water World had ended with five lives lost. Four drowned, and one fell to his death by getting thrown off a cliff by the rushing water and landing on a cluster of jagged rocks. As tragic as it was, it could have been much worse, considering just north of two hundred people were involved. Two more people had lost their lives to the overconsumption of the energy-draining Wacky Water. One was an adult; the other a ninth-grader from Force-Pointe High.

When we heard the news, it was just James and I in Dr. Gabrielle's office. Kelly and Nick were both at the organization's hospital getting treated. According to Dr. Stephani, they were going to be okay, which was a huge relief.

Just like the mutant bug infestation at Force-Pointe High, everything pertaining to Wacky Water seemed to be wiped from the general population's memory. Every last bottle of the stuff had vanished, and the waterpark had cleaned itself up, in a matter of speaking. All that remained was the actual water bottling plant, which had suffered so much water damage it had been condemned. As for the memories of the islanders, Dr. Gabrielle was silent on the matter when James asked her about it. What she did say was that F.E.S.P.A. seemed to vanish the second Wacky Water did.

"So, what do we do now?" James asked.

Dr. Gabrielle looked at him and smiled warmly. "What did you do after your last two missions?"

He lowered his head. "This time is very different. The whole island just forgot about an entire disaster that claimed seven lives. Five they blamed on some kind of freak accident at an illegal rave at the old water factory, the other two simple cases of hypothermia…on a tropical island."

She sighed. "Perhaps it's better that everyone forgets. It would be hard for them to grasp what really happened. I mean, did you guys take the whole Corrupted issue gracefully when you were told?"

James and I looked at each other and shrugged.

"Not exactly," I said. "I'm still trying to get used to it."

"Imagine a few million people learning about this stuff, or trying to rationalize it," said Dr. Gabrielle.

"I suppose you have a point," said James. He frowned. "But we haven't really had to deal with lives lost before. I mean, there were the people that the Illusion Tree drained the life out of, but there was nothing we could have done to stop it. This time, there may have been—"

"You did the best you could do," Dr. Gabrielle interrupted. "You'll drive yourselves crazy beating yourself up over this. There really was nothing else that could have been done."

I looked at my phone; the background was me and Kelly at the mall. We were both cross-eyed looking at the camera, both trying to blow the biggest bubble we could with our gum. That had been a great day. We'd hauled Nick and James around the mall with all of our stuff, and we made Nick take the picture. "We almost lost Nick, and we could have lost Kelly, too."

Dr. Gabrielle stood up from her little chair. "You could have, yes. But you didn't."

"But what about next time?" James asked. "What if next time we *do* lose someone on the team?"

"Don't worry so much about the future," Dr. Gabrielle said calmly.

"That is much easier said than done…" James muttered. "Nick almost died, and if it weren't for that strange man sending us into Marina's dimension, Abby and Kelly would have perished as well."

Dr. Gabrielle turned around. "Yes, I suppose we should thank him."

"Who is he, anyway?" James asked. "He never did give us a name, and he saved us twice now."

Dr. Gabrielle turned toward us and shrugged. "I'm not entirely sure myself. I've only seen him a handful of times. He always says hi to me, and he knows my name. When I asked my dad before he passed, he said that he was a freelance agent that has some pretty unique Segols."

James had a look of fascination on his face. "Segols, as in plural? Like Kelly does?"

Dr. Gabrielle nodded. "Yes. All I know is that he has more than one. The weird thing is, I haven't been able to copy them."

"Well, whoever he is…he does deserve our gratitude," James said.

"Come now," she said with a grin. "Enough of the solemn talk. Aside from the unfortunate losses, this is a victory. You managed to defeat Marina, thus saving countless more lives. And we collected the Ark. Now we have two."

I pulled the Ark out of my purse and looked at it. Its smooth, metallic surface glimmered under the fluorescent lights. The sapphire seemed to glow with a subtle but tangible power.

"Now you should be able to control that time-freezing ability of yours a little better, Abby." Dr. Gabrielle told me.

"That *is* a major relief…" I said. "I was getting tired of accidently Freeze-Framing my classmates all the time."

She laughed, which I didn't know was possible. "Yes, well, now we can call this assignment case closed. You may go."

James and I walked out of Dr. Gabrielle's office. It was raining heavily outside. I could hear the pitter-patter of raindrops as they struck the building. Funny, it really reflected how I felt. I was totally excited that soon my Freeze-Frame ability would be less stressful…but the feeling of sorrow trumped that. Nick had almost died because of me…and that's not the half of it. Five people *did* die because of me. Because of how we beat Marina, it endangered the lives of more than two hundred people when her illusion fell apart.

A little ray of sunshine, though. Kelly and Nick were both released the next day. Kelly was more or less back to normal right away. She was able to go back to school the day after she was discharged. Nick, on the other hand, still had some recovering to do. Dr. Stephani told us that we needed to let him get as much rest as he required. He missed four whole days of school, and basically slept the entire time, occasionally getting up to get some water or go to the bathroom. One night, he actually sleepwalked to the fridge and ate everything in sight. It scared me half to death! I screamed when I saw him sitting at the table, devouring a piece of leftover pizza. He didn't even look up. He didn't even know I was there!

The day after that, James and Kelly came over after school. The three of us were drenched; it had consistently rained the entire week.

"How's he doing?" Kelly asked anxiously.

"He's fine!" I said as I rolled my eyes and smiled. "He just sleeps all day long and occasionally sleepwalks to the fridge and raids it. Nothing completely out of the ordinary."

Kelly managed a half-smile, but I could tell how worried she was. Truth be told, I was too.

James placed a tower of papers and notebooks on the table. "He has almost an entire week of homework to catch up on," he said, adjusting his glasses. "Luckily, I took rather extensive notes for him in biology and history, and I gathered his homework material from his other classes. I sorted them, too. He should have no problem catching up."

I laughed. "Do you really think he's going to do any of that?"

He shrugged. "No, but I did it anyway."

"Just your way of caring for him," said Kelly.

A low growl came from down the hall.

"Abby, what was that?" Kelly asked, frightened.

"Oh, it's probably just—" *Grrrrrr…*

"What if it's a Corrupted planning a surprise attack?" James asked, anxiously.

He and Kelly quickly scrambled down the hall. I giggled as I followed them.

They both opened the door that the noise was coming from, which was Nick's room. They both sighed with relief.

It was just as I expected. Nick was lying sideways across his bed. He was wearing a gray tank top and a pair of red gym shorts, and was snoring away; a little bit of drool dripped out of his mouth and onto his beard.

"Does he usually snore this loudly?" James asked.

I nodded. "Yup, my brother the foghorn."

Kelly walked over to the bed and sat down on it. She looked at him with amusement. "I think it's kinda cute."

Suddenly, Nick sat up. "Thank you," he said drearily.

Kelly started to get up, but Nick suddenly flopped forward and landed on her. Their faces were touching.

"Miss Kelly?" he whispered.

Kelly turned a brand-new shade of red. "Y-yes, Nick?"

"I think he's still asleep," I said.

"Will…you…" he murmured.

"Will I…what?" she asked. Their faces were still touching.

"Will…you…sew my favorite shirt back together, please?"

There was a long pause. Kelly finally opened her mouth. *"Sew?"* she repeated, sounding insulted. She pushed him off of her and slapped him across the face.

He fell back on his pillow and grabbed his cheek. "Yowch, what was that for?" he cried.

Kelly stood up. "Oh, look, he's awake!" She stormed out of the room.

Nick rubbed his cheek. "What was that all about?"

"Apparently, she has an aversion to sewing," James said.

Nick looked at him, perplexed. "Huh?"

I sighed. "Way to ruin a touching moment, bro!" I said crossing my arms.

He blinked at me. "I don't understand what's going on. Did I miss something?"

"Yes," James said. "Four days of school."

He looked shocked "Four days? Wait…does that mean I missed the first basketball game of the season?"

James nodded. "Indeed, and four days of schoolwork. Don't worry, though, I brought everything you need to catch up."

Nick looked crestfallen. Though, I was sure it was about the basketball game and not the schoolwork. Then his eyes widened as if he just remembered something. "Wait, what happened with the water lady?" he said.

"We beat her," I said. "Don't you remember?"

"But it was not all good news…" James said with a frown. "Five people lost their lives at Wacky Water World, and two died from drinking too much Wacky Water."

He was silent for a long moment. Then he struck his fist on the bed. "How…could that many people die?"

"It isn't all bad news, though," I said, trying to sound cheery. "We did get the Ark, and we saved a lot more people from Marina and her Wacky Water."

He looked away from us. "That still doesn't make me feel better. All this was going on and I was taking a nap!"

"You were out of energy and running dangerously low on Edaniite," James said softly.

"You did your part, Nick," I said. "If it wasn't for you, we'd be dead, and so would a lot more people."

He didn't answer for a moment. Finally, he said, "Just…gimme a sec, will ya? I need to be alone for a minute." His voice was broody, almost depressed.

James and I left the room to join Kelly in the family room.

"Hmph, who does he think I am, his mother?" Kelly said, fiddling with her hair, her face still red.

"He was asleep," I said, trying to keep the laughter in.

"Yeah, well…what a stupid dream to have!" she said, smiling a little. "Still, I'm glad he's okay."

"We all are," I said with gratitude.

"What do you say we all go celebrate?" James suggested.

Kelly and I looked at him with disbelief.

"What?" he said, suddenly withdrawing. "I…know how to have fun, too. We can go to the library and have a study party."

"*Gag!*" Nick hacked as he walked out of his room. "I think I'd rather be comatose again."

"What do you suggest, then, brother?" James asked.

"Brother?" I repeated.

"James, you never use nicknames…" Kelly said with surprise. "Well, except for the Hyena Gang."

James smiled. "It is not a nickname. He *is* my brother."

"I'm lost," I said, looking at Nick. "Did we just adopt him or something?"

Nick walked over to James and slapped him on the back. "No, it's a guy thing. You wouldn't understand."

"Okay?" I answered.

"Now, what exactly are we going to do?" Kelly said.

"Let's go shoot some hoops!" Nick suggested. "J-Man's gotta practice his game, anyway. Isn't that right?"

James scratched his cheek and looked away from Nick's gaze. "I would, but I am afraid I hurt my hand during our latest mission. Would not be good to strain it. Besides, you should still take it easy!"

He sighed. "I've been taking it easy for four days, right?"

"Why don't we just go to the arcade?" Kelly suggested.

"I'm game," I said.

"I suppose I can attempt a better score on Street Fighter," said James.

"Not if I kick your butt first, J-Man!" Nick said cheerily.

"I hope you know I am the best Street Fighter player on the Force-Pointe Islands," James said proudly.

Nick chided him. "Psh, that's because you haven't fought me yet!"

"Before we go there," said Kelly. We all looked at her. "We should go to the mall to look at shoes! I need to get a new pair since my favorite tennis shoes got ruined from the sea hag."

"Ooh, I need to get a new pair, too!" I said, excited.

Nick and James groaned in disappointment.

"Why do you always have'ta do that?" Nick said with his shoulders down. "Can't we ever just go to the arcade?"

James sighed. "I agree—"

Kelly gave James the death glare.

"—with Kelly, of course," James said nervously.

"Hey, I thought we were brothers!" said Nick. "You're supposed to have *my* back!"

"In most cases," James said, slouching. "But you don't want to make Kelly mad."

He rubbed his cheek; it was still rosy from her slap. "I heard that!"

"So, it's settled?" Kelly said, with a victorious grin.

And out we went for a night of shopping and fun. It was still raining when we left, and it would rain for the next two weeks. By the time it stopped, our next encounter with the Corrupted would begin.

# THE ADVENTURE CONTINUES
# EDANIA CHRONICLES BOOK 4: THE CRESCENT MOON GANG

What happens when the Corrupted employ an average criminal gang to help them find an Ark? Kidnappings. Disappearances. Potential murder. All this, and Abby and the others are forbidden to use their Segols to harm a normal person, no matter how evil they are.

What will the team do when one of their own goes missing? How can they fight an entire gang of criminals without using their powers? To top it all off, they've got to search an entire abandoned amusement park to find the Ark and their missing teammate. And a powerful Corrupted is dwelling in the shadows, watching everything unfold. Waiting for the moment when he can get the Ark.

# ABOUT THE AUTHOR

Matthew Porter is the author of the Edania Chronicles, a series about friendship, secret organizations, and superpowers. He lives in a small town right outside of Columbus Ohio. In his free time, he likes to spend time with his family and friends. His interests include Jewish history and infectious diseases. His library includes books on Jewish culture and religion; handbooks on writing; and textbooks on microbiology, immunology, epidemiology, and other "ologies" that pertain to germs and how our bodies fight them.

He is a member of the Indie Wordsmiths, a group of four authors that offer clean, quality fiction for your literary needs. You'll find stories about romance, coming of age, fairies, dragons, superheroes, and friendship. Check out the links below for more information on Matthew Porter and the Indie Wordsmiths, and don't forget to sign up for our newsletter for the latest information on our books, promotions and freebies:
Facebook page: https://www.facebook.com/author.matthewporter
Author website: https://matthewporterauthor.com/
Indie Wordsmiths: https://www.subscribepage.com/indiewordsmiths